MW01199948

CHARMED BY THE COWBOY

A CONTEMPORARY CHRISTIAN ROMANCE

BLACKWATER RANCH SERIES
BOOK TWO

MANDI BLAKE

Charmed by the Cowboy
Blackwater Ranch Book 2
By Mandi Blake
All Rights Reserved

Copyright © 2020 Mandi Blake
All Rights Reserved

Published in the United States of America
Cover Designer: Amanda Walker PA & Design Services
Editor: Editing Done Write
Ebook ISBN: 978-1-7344302-6-4
Paperback ISBN: 978-1-7344302-7-1

CONTENTS

CHAPTER 1

MADDIE

"You can do this," Maddie whispered to herself as she turned left at the rusted Blackwater Ranch sign. "You've survived everything so far. You can handle this too. God is with you."

Her pep-talks tended to all be the same, but it sounded less creepy and weird when Dolly was around for some reason. Talking to a horse was more acceptable than talking to yourself.

Maddie Faulkner had dreamed about this day, but she never thought it would arrive. She checked her rearview mirror, hoping the horse trailer didn't land in the culvert.

Once on the straightaway, she rubbed a sweaty palm on her jeans. What if this was a trap?

No, the Hardings weren't the conniving kind. Anita Harding had sounded as sweet during the phone interview last week as Maddie remembered from her childhood. If that call could even be considered an interview. It had been a job offer on the spot.

Maddie brushed a hand over her brow and down the braid that hung over her left shoulder. The Hardings hadn't deserved what happened to them the last time she'd been here. Would anyone remember her? Did any of them know what her parents had done? If Anita knew, she sure hadn't let on during the phone call.

Maddie couldn't believe the Hardings were letting her come back. It had been fifteen years since she'd stepped foot onto Blackwater Ranch, and she'd missed it with all of her heart. The ranch had been the only place she'd wanted to call home. Later, she'd realized it was just one more stop in a line of endless moves.

From Boise to Twin Falls to Jackson to Blackwater, there were few places she'd stayed in her early life for more than a couple of years. Some stops had been so temporary that her family hadn't bothered to unpack.

The Faulkners had landed at Blackwater Ranch when Maddie was eight years old—not even old enough or smart enough to guard her heart from the impending break. If she'd known her parents would uproot her in a year and a half, would she have been able to enjoy the best time of her life here? Probably not.

Would she see Lucas and Asher? It was possible they still worked the ranch. Blackwater had always been a generational operation, and the Harding boys had loved working with their dad, Silas.

Her heart rate rose at the thought of seeing Lucas Harding. She wondered if he had changed. He'd been cute when they were kids, but she'd been wildly drawn to his free spirit.

Maddie chuckled to herself. Of course Lucas had changed. She hadn't seen him since he was eight years old. He was probably married by now, and, besides, she wasn't here to rekindle her old crush. She'd lost any hope of finding some kind of lifetime, over-the-moon love when she was still in middle school—when her world had fallen apart.

But, first, she had to find Asher. He'd been like a big brother to her when she was young. Should she just waltz up and tell him that her parents had schemed and plotted for months and ultimately stolen who-knows-what from his family before packing up and leaving in the middle of the night?

Maddie swallowed hard, knowing she wasn't brave enough to put it all out in the open like that. She'd learned how to hide her true emotions years ago with practiced expressions and squared shoulders. But on the inside, she was a timid mess.

It was harder than ever to hold her head high when she wore shame like a weight on her back. Her time here at Blackwater Ranch had shaped her into the person she was today. She hadn't kept up with any of the Hardings after she'd left, but she remembered some of them. Mama Harding made the best cookies, and Asher has been a quirky brother-like figure who looked after her.

Lucas was another story. Her feelings for him had been jumbled at best when her nine-year-old self had left Blackwater Ranch under the cover of darkness. How many times had he gotten her into trouble when they were kids? If her mother told her not to get muddy, he'd splash her clothes and laugh. She knew now that it'd all been fun and games to the playful little boy. How could he have known the tongue lashing she'd get when she had to ride home in her mother's car covered in dried mud?

She'd had enough fun with Lucas in her short time at Blackwater Ranch to last her a lifetime. In the years after leaving Blackwater, Maddie realized that all Lucas had done for her was get her in trouble with her parents and leave her young heart raw and open for the breaking.

Before leaving the Kellerman Hotel this morning, she'd prayed for composure and plastered on her confident smile. If she couldn't feel confident, she at least needed to make people think she was. How long her brave face held today depended on who she encountered first. Right now, she was holding it together with masking tape and a prayer.

Her trusty diesel pickup had the dust swirling

behind her as she barreled up the long drive toward the main house. The two-story log home hadn't changed a bit. She remembered everything about this place from the layout of the rooms to the smell of Mama Harding's oatmeal raisin cookies to the storage house out back where she used to meet Lucas after school to play in the stables.

The land closest to Blackwater was gently rolling hills, but rugged mountains surrounded the wide-open expanse. This place was different from the Appalachian foothills in every way. The Tennessee mountains that she'd just left were rolling and green compared to the jutting Tetons and the gray Bighorn Mountains.

She parked in the open area in front of the main house and checked on Dolly as the dust settled. Traveling across the country with a horse wasn't the easiest, so she'd planned plenty of stops. "How's my girl?" Maddie brushed her hand down the mare's neck. "You're gonna love it here."

Dolly had been with Maddie since she was sixteen. They'd barrel raced with the best of them in their hay day, but the old girl was getting past her prime.

Maddie pulled a treat from a bag in the bed of the truck and offered it to the horse. Dolly was her heart horse—the animal she'd formed an unspoken understanding with that would forever be precious to her.

They'd made a quick stop at the hotel where Maddie would be staying this morning before heading on into the ranch. She'd gotten up before sunrise to drive the last stretch, and Dolly needed to get out of the trailer soon. Maddie looked toward the main house before resting her head against the cool metal of the horse trailer.

"Dear Lord, please give me the strength to face them today. I need peace like only You can give me. Please calm my heart and sharpen my focus." She whispered the last words. "I want to stay here no matter what happened last time."

Lifting her head, she bit the inside of her cheek. It was dangerous to hope for a home after twenty-three years without one, but she was a glutton for punishment. At the very least, she had a job, and that was more than she'd had last week.

Letting her hand slip from Dolly's mane, she made her way toward the main house. Anita Harding opened the door just as an excited border collie darted around the house and bounded onto the porch. Maddie reached down to quickly rustle the dog's head.

"Good morning, Maddie." Anita held out her arms for an embrace instead of a cordial handshake. "It's good to see you again. You've grown so much."

Taken aback by the familiar greeting, Maddie stepped into the hug and wrapped one arm around the woman's waist. When was the last time she'd been shown affection by someone other than Aunt Brenda?

"It's good to see you too, Mrs. Harding."

The matriarch of the Harding family hadn't changed much in the years they'd been apart. Her black hair was now streaked with gray, but her eyes held a kindness that Maddie almost mistook for innocence. It was impossible and thoughtless of her to think so. She knew Anita hadn't lived an easy life. She'd raised five boys, been robbed by Maddie's parents, and Maddie remembered talk of a fire that had devastated the ranch not long before she'd come to live there herself.

Such was the life on a Wyoming cattle ranch. You had to dry your eyes and press on through the tough times if you wanted the privilege of experiencing the good times.

Anita released the hug and patted Maddie's shoulder. "You can call me Mama Harding. Most everyone else does."

Maddie nodded and her smile grew. Maybe things would be better than she'd thought at Blackwater Ranch. Why had she been so nervous this morning?

Mama Harding waved Maddie into the main house and gestured to the long row of boot racks. "If your boots are dirty, you can just leave them here. If they're wet, you can hang them up."

Inside, the meeting room looked exactly the

same as it had almost fifteen years ago. The stained wood walls and rustic light fixtures were casual and inviting. The long tables were empty, but Maddie recalled this room full and bustling with excitement at meal times in her childhood.

Mama Harding pointed toward three rows of hooks just inside the door. "You can hang your hat here."

Maddie hung her ivory cowboy hat on an open hook and followed Mama Harding.

"You remember the meeting room. Breakfast is thirty minutes before sunrise, lunch is at noon, and supper is at half past six every evening. If you miss it, you're on your own."

A tall older man stepped into the room followed by a young boy who couldn't be older than three. Maddie recognized the man as Silas Harding, Anita's husband.

"Maddie. I heard you were comin'." He extended a hand in greeting. "We're glad to have you here."

"I'm glad to be back, Mr. Harding."

Mama Harding held out an open hand to the boy, and he rushed to grab it. "This here's Levi. Aaron's boy. He hangs around with us sometimes while his dad works."

Maddie let her mask dissolve and revealed a genuine smile for the boy. "Hey, Levi. Nice to meet you."

Levi gave her a small wave as he clung to Mama

Harding's hand with his. "Hey." His eyes were a dark green like his father's and grandfather's.

Maddie would find out what the Harding brothers looked like now, but she remembered small features about each of them. They could be divided by their eye colors and linked back to one parent. Noah, Lucas, and Asher shared the rich brown eyes of their mother, while Micah, Aaron, and now Levi, had Silas's emerald eyes.

Silas pulled his wife in close with one arm and kissed the side of her head. "I'm taking Levi to the feed and seed. We'll be back soon."

Maddie watched as Levi followed Silas out the back door and felt a tiny pull in her chest. Levi was lucky to have a family who cared about him.

"Have a seat." Mama Harding gestured to the table. "I'll be right back with the forms you need to sign."

Maddie studied the meeting room as she took the first seat at the table and rubbed the tips of her fingers over the grooves and knots in the wood. She could do this. She needed this job. Dolly needed a place where she could have room to roam with other horses. And, most of all, Maddie needed a home.

Shaking her head, she pressed the pad of her finger into the jagged edge of a splinter in the wood. Thoughts like that would get her in trouble.

Mama Harding returned with a few papers and a

pen. She passed the loose forms to Maddie and indicated a few places she should sign.

While Maddie sealed her position at the ranch, Mama Harding told her a little about the general operations. When she started talking about the horses, Maddie eased the pen to the table and listened intently. She'd found her love of horses here, and it lifted her spirits to be back. A lot had happened since her time here, but one thing hadn't changed. Horses were her life, and her life was horses.

Out of all the places Maddie had lived over the years, if there had ever been one she'd secretly wished she could call home, it was Blackwater Ranch. Leaving the first time had broken her young, innocent heart.

Maddie had to keep her guard up this time. It was just a job, and sometimes jobs didn't work out. Getting her hopes up that she would be able to stay here was a surefire way to ensure she was left hurting again when things didn't pan out. After all, if she hadn't found her resting place in her first twenty-three years, what kind of hope did she have of finding it now?

"We can fix up a cabin for you if you'd like to stay on the property," Mama Harding explained. "Housing wouldn't be an extra charge, but just know that there isn't anything fancy like TV or the internet. You can only find those things here at the main house."

"I'm sold. Where do I sign for the free living quarters?" Maddie jested.

Mama Harding waved her hand. "I'll get the boys on it. They can probably have it livable in a few weeks."

"That's great. I'm staying at the Kellerman Hotel, but I'd prefer to be closer to Dolly."

Mama Harding smiled. "Dolly has a place here too. If you have any questions about getting her settled in, you can ask Lucas. He spends the most time with the horses."

Maddie tensed at the mention of Lucas's name. She'd been foolish to think she could avoid him. He was her boss now, and the only thing she should be concerned with was letting him know she was a trustworthy, reliable worker.

Mama Harding stood before Maddie had a chance to relax. "Let's go. He should be here any minute, and he'll help you and Dolly get settled in."

Maddie squared her shoulders and schooled the protective mask over her panic. She would face Lucas Harding with a smile, and she prayed she could forget about her old feelings for him and keep her new job.

CHAPTER 2
LUCAS

Lucas stared at the text from his mother.
She's here.

It was eight in the morning, but he'd been up since four. He hadn't slept much at all last night. His mind had been too full of wonderings about the new woman his parents had hired to help care for the horses.

Lucas whistled high and sharp to get his brother's attention, and Vader shook his head. The stallion was as easily excitable as Lucas, and that made them a good pair.

Micah didn't move his focus from the herd funneling into the adjacent pasture. "Yeah?"

"I gotta go meet the new horse hand," Lucas shouted and pointed toward the main house. "You good here, or you need me to call Noah?"

Micah craned his neck to shout over his shoulder. "Nah. I got it."

Lucas didn't wait around for any extra commentary from his older brother. Micah was already focused back on his task.

Spurring the black stallion into a gallop, Lucas let the excitement build in his middle as the cool wind whooshed past him. His mom had refused to tell him anything about the new hire, claiming he'd have no problem working with her and he needed to meet her before worrying about her resume. His dad had been tight-lipped too, and Lucas was certain his mom had her hand in the silence.

The secrecy had frustrated him at first, but his anticipation had now turned to eagerness. Lucas was a go-getter, and sitting on his hands wasn't on his list of things to do. Instead of dwelling on his unanswered questions about his new co-worker, he'd thrown himself into work this last week.

Unfortunately, there wasn't anything to keep the wonderings at bay in the quiet hours of the night. Lucas might be a carefree guy, but the horses were important to him. He didn't trust them with just anyone. His brothers knew plenty about horses, but that came with the territory when you grew up on a ranch. It was in their blood.

A stranger might be able to fool his parents into believing they knew the difference in a quarter horse and a thoroughbred, but Lucas would see through her act if she wasn't the real McCoy.

What if she was a stubborn, wiry-haired grandma who wouldn't listen to him because he was young and liked to joke around? The last thing he needed was a stick-in-the-mud cramping his style in the stable.

He was getting really tired of defending his God-given right to be happy. Why did it irritate some people that he was friendly? It tended to be the older folks who scrunched up their noses at him. Hadn't they ever heard the saying "work hard, play hard?"

That really wasn't his problem though, and he wasn't gonna let Grumpy Granny push him around. He knew his way around the stables better than anyone, and he wasn't going down without a fight.

Lucas urged Vader on as they crested the last rise before the main house. Despite his worry over the new ranch hand, it was a good thing they were hiring someone to help with the horses. He couldn't keep it up on his own anymore, and his brothers all had their hands full with other ranch duties. He didn't want the horses to be neglected while he worked his weekly forty-eight-hour shifts at the fire station.

What in the world?

The old white Chevy parked next to the main house was hauling a horse trailer. Mom and Dad definitely hadn't mentioned adding another horse to the stables. His anxiety turned to excitement at the thought of learning a new horse. Each animal was unique, just like a person, and Lucas had learned to bond with them depending on their personality.

He pulled Vader to a stop, jumped off the horse, and made a beeline for the trailer. A chestnut quarter horse pressed the side of her face against the metal.

"Hey there." The horse sniffed his offered hand. "I'm Lucas."

Most of the horses in the stable were quarter horses. Was she a cutting horse? There was a chance she was a barrel racer. She was well fed, and her coat was shiny, indicating a good feed and caretaker.

"I'll be back. Gotta see a woman about a horse." Lucas affectionately patted the horse's neck.

"There you are." His mother rounded the side of the trailer with a mischievous smile on her face.

Lucas's attention was drawn to the woman accompanying his mother. For once, he was speechless.

Her long blonde braid rested over one shoulder, framing the side of her pale, heart-shaped face. Her jaw was angled to a feminine chin, and her thin lips and button nose gave her a youthful air.

But those eyes. They were green with a hazy sea-glass tint that had him stepping closer, lost in a trance.

"Lucas, this is Maddie Faulkner. Maddie, you remember Lucas."

"Remember?" he questioned. Where were his manners? "I mean, it's a pleasure to meet you. Have we met?" he asked, extending his hand to her.

No, he was sure they hadn't met. He would never forget those eyes.

Maddie grasped his hand with a guarded smile, and Lucas was surprised that it wasn't as smooth as he expected. Brownie points to the newcomer. Calloused hands were working hands. His smile grew. Oh, he was eager to get to know her and got the impression she knew what she was doing. Her horse, her calloused hands, and her pristine posture were good indicators of her know-how.

"Many years ago. I appreciate the opportunity to work with the horses here."

"Glad to have you."

She'd dodged details in his question about knowing him, but he'd let it slide for now. He had plenty of time to find out later.

"I think we're all set here. Why don't you two head on over to the stable and get Dolly settled in?" His mother shooed them off.

Dolly. Interesting name.

"Sure, you can follow me over with the trailer," Lucas said.

Maddie nodded, but her expression remained lifeless.

"See you two for lunch," Mama Harding called over her shoulder as she walked back toward the house.

"So, Dolly?" Lucas asked as they moved around the trailer.

"Yeah."

"How long have you had her?"

Maddie tilted her head toward the sun before donning her cowboy hat. "Almost eight years."

After a moment, when she didn't offer anything else, Lucas frowned. Was he going to have to ask every question to get the whole story? "Is she a cuttin' horse?"

"No, we barrel raced when I was in high school. She's past her prime now, though."

A few more beats of silence prompted Lucas to offer another question. "Where are you from?" He stopped beside the trailer to check on Dolly one last time before they made their way over to the stable.

"Franklin, Tennessee."

He should have guessed from the slight southern twang in her voice. "Ah, so, Dolly Parton?"

"So, Dolly Parton," Maddie confirmed.

Was he seeing things, or was she trying not to crack a smile?

Lucas's attention went back to the horse, but he was hopeful he might have lightened the mood with his witty comment.

"The stables and horse pastures are just over that hill." He gestured to the closest rise.

"Got it." Maddie climbed into her Chevy without a backward glance at him.

Sheesh. She was a tough cookie. Getting more than one- or two-word answers from her was like pulling teeth. Why did that make her all the more mysterious and intriguing?

Lucas mounted Vader and led the way to the stables. She parked in front of the stable, and he watched her take in the reaches of the pastures.

"Has she eaten?" Lucas asked as he approached the trailer.

"She gets fed in the evenings, but I bet she's just ready to get out. We've been on the road for a few days."

Lucas waited while Maddie led Dolly out of the trailer. They trotted over to him, and he patted the horse's side again before pointing toward the pastures.

"We're standing in the south pasture, and that up there is the north pasture. That's where we keep the rougher horses that don't get along so well. This is Vader, and that bay over there is Blane. They're stallions and fail at working well with others, so sometimes they take turns in the pasture. The others are friendlier and never cause trouble. They love each other."

Lucas grinned and rubbed Dolly's neck. "I bet you're a lover, not a fighter."

Dolly nuzzled closer to him, and Maddie revealed her first true expression—outrage.

Lucas waited for her to say something—anything that was on her mind. She was probably feisty beneath the mask.

When Maddie schooled her features and relaxed, disappointment hung on his shoulders. They'd only been together for a few minutes, but she'd been so closed off that he didn't know how to find out anything about her.

Focus on the horses.

Moving on, he showed her where to find everything from grooming supplies to feed and snacks to the tack room before giving her a key to the stable office. He explained the pastures and gates, while she groomed Dolly. Maddie didn't say much while Lucas talked, other than an occasional "Mmhmm" or "okay."

When Dolly was ready, they led her back outside to the pasture. Lucas introduced them to each horse. There were seven on the ranch, not counting the newcomer.

He watched as Maddie's stoic demeanor softened around the animals, and he relaxed a fraction. He'd been wondering if she would be the right person for the job. The horses meant a lot to him, and he wasn't about to leave them with someone who didn't care.

As they walked through the pasture, he explained the job duties and when everything should happen, but Maddie's expression didn't so much as twitch once they were away from the horses.

Was she uncomfortable around him? She seemed fine with the horses. He wanted to catch another glimpse of the smile she'd given the animals.

"Your mom didn't ask for my qualifications. I'm sure you have questions for me," Maddie finally spoke up.

"You mean, for your interview? Yeah, Mom isn't big on formalities," he said, brushing it off as no big deal.

Maddie raised an eyebrow, as if waiting for him to grill her.

He could play along to appease her. "If you were part of a pencil, would you be the lead or the eraser?" Lucas asked as he leaned against the wooden wall.

"What?"

"You wanted interview questions. I happen to think your answer to this one will provide me with information I need to know about you."

Her lips squished together to contain a reaction. "The lead."

"Why?"

Maddie's brows furrowed in concentration. "Because if you do something correctly the first time, you don't need the eraser."

Her answer said perfectionist, and a wave of unease crept into his shoulders. How would she react to a change in plans or getting a horse ready for a job on short notice?

"Next question. If you were a fruit, which one would you be?"

She thought for a few seconds longer on this question. "Okay, I would be a watermelon."

Intrigued, Lucas asked, "Why?"

She shifted her weight to the other foot and averted her gaze as she thought. "Because I'm not the same on the outside as I am on the inside."

Lucas didn't pry further, but he hoped she meant tough on the outside and sweet on the inside. "Fair enough. You passed the test. Do you still feel like you've been cheated out of the full interview experience?"

"No, I'm sure you'll see my qualifications as I work." Her confident posture showed Lucas she thought she could handle whatever he threw at her.

He then remembered his mother's introduction earlier. "Did Mom say you would remember me? Should I know you?"

He'd thought about it for a fleeting moment back at the main house, but he hadn't been able to come up with a Maddie Faulkner in his memory. She was beautiful, and he was sure he would have remembered her.

Maddie shrugged but didn't make eye contact with him. "It was a long time ago. We were really young."

"Like, were we crawling, or were we avoiding cooties?" Lucas asked.

The corner of Maddie's lip twitched. "Avoiding cooties."

"Ah. There's a chance I put a garter snake in your boots at some point." Lucas leaned against the stall door and grinned at her. "Mama about beat me silly one summer."

Maddie kept her chin tucked, but he was certain he'd seen an upturn at the corner of her mouth.

Lucas swallowed hard. If he kept focusing on her mouth, he'd find himself in trouble. Maddie was beautiful, and he'd have to be blind not to notice her.

"If it wasn't a snake, it might have been a chick." Lucas rubbed a hand over his chin. "I'm the reason we don't have fowl on the ranch anymore."

Maddie shook her head and met his gaze. "No, nothing like that. I think I've got things here. Thanks for showing me around."

She stepped around him, placing the hoof pick in its place. So much for getting to know her. Lucas might be wishing for grouchy grandma before this was over.

"Right. I'll be back before lunch to pick you up."

Maddie hollered over her shoulder. "I have my truck. I'll just meet you there."

Lucas stared at her for a few moments, contemplating the unfairness. All of his luck had been used up in getting a gorgeous assistant. There wasn't any left for friendliness.

"Suit yourself, Miss Maddie. I'll see you at lunch." Tipping his hat in farewell, he slowed his steps as he left her behind in the stable, just in case she changed her mind.

She didn't, and Lucas was left wondering if there was something about *him* that was putting her off. He rarely had trouble making a friend, and he was a little concerned about the insincere smile she flashed him too often.

The connections between people always interested him. He'd learned early in life that if he gave someone his full attention, they were generally more comfortable talking to him. It seemed like the right thing to do—listen to someone. A strong handshake and eye contact had served him well over the years.

However, none of his usual conversation powers had worked on Maddie. She'd dismissed him without a second thought.

He greeted Vader as he slung his leg over the antsy horse. Before riding off to finish the shelving in the north barn with Micah, Lucas cast one more glance at the stable. He'd be spending a lot of time with Maddie. Maybe he shouldn't be so pushy. After all, they'd just met. She'd open up to him when she was ready. At least, that was the hope.

Lucas nudged Vader into a gallop and made his way to help his brother. He knew women were just as capable of working the ranch as the men were. His brother's new fiancée, Camille, was quickly learning the ropes and helping out when she could.

What would it be like working with Maddie? He'd have to wait to find out since she'd pushed him out the door.

How would he and the mysterious Maddie Faulkner be able to work together? She seemed closed off and reserved, whereas he was lively and outgoing.

They would have to find a way to make it work. He was determined to find the truth behind that false smile.

CHAPTER 3
MADDIE

Meeting Lucas had been more nerve-wracking than Maddie had anticipated, and her skin stayed sweaty and clammy until lunchtime. She'd have to ask Mama Harding if she could wear T-shirts during the summer. There hadn't been any talk of a dress code.

Maddie had just finished grooming Sprite when her stomach growled. She pursed her lips and debated skipping lunch at the main house with the whole crew, but she hadn't brought anything to eat, and it was a long time till supper. She was prone to hangry outbursts if left unfed, so she dusted off her jeans, tightened her braid, and headed to face the music.

Three trucks were already parked at the entrance when she reached the main house, and she didn't hesitate to head inside. A moment of indecision would take away any confidence she'd formed.

Dixie met her at the truck, hyper and begging for a scratch.

"Hey, girl." Maddie scratched the border collie's head and patted her side.

She removed her boots and placed them neatly beside the other pairs lining the wall next to the door. With her painted smile firmly in place, she entered the meeting room for her first meal with the Hardings.

Thankfully, she wasn't late. Stepping in to meet a handful of founding family members beat a grand entrance in front of the whole herd. Mama Harding smiled and quickly waved before turning her attention back to the food she was placing on the serving counter.

"Hello, dear," Mama Harding called out from across the room. "Just hang around for a bit. We'll get started in a few."

The three men turned their attention to her and promptly made their way to meet her with handshakes and introductions.

The first man was stout with broad shoulders and green eyes. Maddie remembered Micah from when they were kids. He hadn't really changed that much since he'd been older when she was here before.

"I'm Micah. Good to see you again, Maddie." His

handshake and greeting were friendly, but his smile was lazy as if he were already tired at noon.

"Same to you, Micah. It's been a while."

She could do this. These people were kind, and she had at least a vague history with most of them. Reminding herself that no one here would bite, she found the courage to show her genuine smile as she met the remaining Hardings.

The next brother had the warm, brown eyes of his mother. "I don't know if you remember me, but I'm Noah." He shook her hand with a friendly smile.

"I do, a little," Maddie admitted. There were a lot of brothers to remember. Five if she recalled correctly.

Another sturdy man with dark hair introduced himself.

"I'm Aaron. I remember you from before. Mom was just telling us you're helping Lucas out with the horses."

With a timid smile, Maddie nodded.

"You'll do a great job. Lucas is easy to work with." Noah nudged her shoulder. It was a brotherly gesture, and Maddie forced her mind not to cling to the camaraderie.

They all heard someone come in and turned their attention toward the door.

Asher threw his cowboy hat at the rack without looking. "Is that Maddie Bug?" His arms were wide open as he strode toward her with a huge grin on his face.

Asher was three years older than Maddie, and he'd taken her under his wing when her mom had managed the books and general operations at the ranch. If anyone at Blackwater could look past what had happened and see Maddie's true intentions, it would be him. He'd been fun and friendly, but he'd also had a level head at the young age of eleven.

Before she'd perfected the mask that protected her from sympathetic questions and pitiful eyes, Asher had once been beside her, building up her confidence as best as a young kid could. He'd taught her to hold her chin up when his brother, Lucas, hadn't returned her innocent feelings. Asher hadn't let his older brothers, Micah and Aaron, leave her out when she wanted to tag along when they went fishing or horseback riding.

"Asher! It's good to see you."

How could she temper her reaction when he was so happy? She tried not to think of the consequences of opening her heart to these people so early. The heartbreak might be inevitable. She'd always liked Asher, but it had been tough to leave her friend all those years ago.

Asher wrapped his arms around her, twirling her around once before setting her back on solid ground. He was built lithe and lean, but he carried her with ease. She'd always trusted Asher. His kind, happy heart didn't understand disloyalty.

"Lucas just told me you're the new horse hand. That's great news!"

At the mention of Lucas's name, Maddie instinctively felt watched. She scanned the room behind Asher to find Lucas staring at her. Shock colored his features as he approached her.

"What is this?" Lucas asked in what seemed to be feigned outrage before turning his attention to her. "I thought we had something special."

Asher laughed. "You didn't even remember her! What a loser."

"I was seven!" Lucas defended.

"You also stuck the ends of her hair in chlorine water when she fell asleep in the hay barn and turned her hair green," Asher reminded Lucas.

Maddie felt a blush creeping up her chest and over her collar. She'd love to forget most of the pranks Lucas had pulled, even the ones where she'd been an accomplice.

Lucas's eyes widened. "Good grief. Why didn't someone beat my tail?"

"I did!" Mama Harding shouted from beyond the open kitchen door.

Asher laughed and slapped a hand on Lucas's back. "You can't win 'em all."

Lucas flashed a smile that sent her stomach flipping. "Who said I was playing a game?"

He winked at her, and his gaze held hers so long that she thought the heat sliding up her spine would melt her insides.

Maddie couldn't breathe. She stood, immobilized, hoping for someone or something to come along and pull her from the trance Lucas had trapped her in.

This was why she'd avoided even glancing his direction all morning. She could be tempted with those eyes, and she could easily feel things that were too great to hope for.

The slamming of the door shocked her from the daydream. A dark-haired man covered in grease strode into the room without greeting anyone.

"That's everyone," Mama Harding shouted. "Wash up and get in line."

Lucas slowed his steps to hang back near Maddie, and she resisted the urge to fan her face. Was it hot in here, or was it just Lucas?

She tried her best not to observe him as he took his place beside her in the line at the washroom. The sleeves of his shirt were rolled up to his elbows, and she discreetly admired his muscular arms.

Turning her back to him, she donned her classic smile. She'd let the facade slip so quickly, and she needed to remember the most important rule about meeting new people: don't get attached.

Lucas leaned in close, and his warm breath

tickled her ear as he whispered, "Doesn't this remind you of the horses' feeding time?"

"Yeah, it does." Maddie bit her lips between her teeth to fight her grin. He'd showed her how the horses were to be fed this morning and explained that there was an order to who ate first. When he called them, the horses lined up in the same order every day. This morning, Sadie had tried to cut the line, but Lucas had righted her with a click behind his teeth.

The whole Harding family lined up to eat, leaving space for Mama Harding to serve herself first.

"No one else gets my horse references," Lucas said quietly behind her.

Maddie felt a tug in her chest—something pulling her toward Lucas. She knew what it was like to always be surrounded by people who didn't understand the role horses played in her life.

She couldn't turn to him. It had only been a few hours, and she was already confusing herself. It was too early to know if her position here at the ranch would work out, and she wasn't ready to tie her heart to a place she might have to leave.

CHAPTER 4
LUCAS

L unch was interesting and only served to confuse Lucas even more.

Apparently, Maddie had some kind of insta-bond with Asher, and Lucas was none too happy about his brother's reaction to their casual closeness.

Lucas frowned at the sprawling field of hay that lay ahead of his baler. He breathed in the smell of drying grass and savored the summer sun as he attempted to calm his unease.

Was this gnawing urge to lock his brother in a full nelson really jealousy? It definitely could be. He'd never wanted to kick Asher in the shin for no good reason before today.

Lucas couldn't stop thinking about the beautiful smile that had lifted Maddie's cheeks when she saw Asher.

Why couldn't she smile like that around him? It seemed as if she had her mind set to temper any reactions toward him. She'd barely even looked his way all morning, and she'd kept her head down at lunch.

Maybe Asher was right. Lucas couldn't win them all, but he'd been honest when he'd said he wasn't playing. Getting to know someone and building a connection wasn't a game to him. He valued his friends, and he had *lots* of friends. In fact, he could name the people he wasn't friends with on one finger—Jameson Ford.

Jameson worked part-time at Blackwater Ranch, and he'd been competing with Lucas since grade school. They'd grown up together, and everything from baseball to grades had been grounds for a match-up.

These days, there was a silent competition between them that Jameson didn't seem to understand. They both had surface reasons they vied for Silas Harding's approval, but Lucas's reasons ran deeper.

Beyond the competitions, their personalities clashed. Jameson was a no-nonsense kinda guy, and he looked down on Lucas's energetic penchant for fun any chance he got.

Lucas turned in the tractor bucket seat to make sure the baler was running straight and tried to forget his qualms with Jameson.

Why couldn't he remember Maddie from when they were kids? Sure, he'd been young, but she was only a year older than him, if what Asher said was true. She remembered him, after all.

When he righted himself in his seat, a flash of a memory gave him pause.

He remembered running through the west field toward the stable. Pumping his arms and panting through a smile, he'd turned to see if the girl chasing him was gaining ground. Blonde hair flew behind her as she ran, and her smile mirrored his own.

Had that been Maddie? Probably not. That girl who'd hung around the ranch for a year or so when her parents had worked here seemed so different from the Maddie he'd met today. That kid had been wide-eyed and always up for one of Lucas's crazy ideas.

That little girl had started the garter snake debacle. He'd been the first one to catch a snake in his boot, and they'd laughed about the prank while she showed him the nest she'd found. Maddie hadn't batted an eye when he'd mentioned the snake pranks earlier today, so it couldn't have been her.

But then again, she'd been so reserved the entire lunch, she might have hidden her reaction to his mention of the snakes. Throughout the whole meal, she'd kept her head down and hadn't said anything other than what was asked of her.

She might just be shy. Lucas couldn't say he

knew much about the reserved personality trait, but he could try his best to make her feel welcome around here. It'd be his fault if he mistook self-consciousness for rudeness.

He had one more chance to make a good first-day impression on Maddie, and failing wasn't on his list of things to do today.

Just before supper, Lucas caught his brother's fiancée, Camille, at the door to the meeting room where everyone congregated for meals.

"Millie! Wait up." Lucas jogged up the steps and caught up to her on the porch.

Camille Vanderbilt had a rigid posture that told of her family wealth, but Lucas knew Millie was one of the good ones. She stood up for what she believed in, and thankfully, she was bonded to Blackwater Ranch just like the Hardings.

Lucas pointed toward the door. "The new horse hand is in there, and I wanted to ask you to be extra nice to her. You're the only woman around here besides Mama, and she might be feeling left out around all these men."

Camille's eyes widened. "The new hire is a woman?"

"Yeah. Her name is Maddie Faulkner. She hasn't given me the time of day yet, but I'm hoping to make a good impression on her tonight."

Camille's eyebrow rose. "Lucas, don't be pushy and scare her off."

"I'm not!" he cried. "I'm just trying to be friendly."

Camille's grin softened as she swiped her hand down the front of his shirt a few times. "I know. It's just that some folks would rather be left alone."

He tucked his chin and checked out his shirt. It was covered in tiny sprigs of hay. "I just want her to like it here. I think she really loves the horses, and that's what we need. I don't want some Joe Schmo who just knows how to keep them alive."

"I get it," Camille said as she opened the door and urged him to follow her. "Come on. I'm hungry, and I promise to be nice so you can keep her."

Camille's acceptance eased the tension in Lucas's shoulders, but when he spotted Maddie talking to Asher across the meeting room, he was on high alert. She was smiling again. What was it about Asher that made her feel comfortable? Lucas was just as friendly and funny. She might figure that out if she looked his way for two seconds.

He made a beeline for her and inserted himself into the small crowd surrounding her.

"How'd everything go today?" He gave her his nicest smile, hoping to foster the same in return.

She hadn't called him with any questions, so unfortunately, his casual question held the undertone of micromanaging.

"It went well." Her smile faded slowly as she spoke, but it didn't disappear completely. "Sprite and Dolly are sticking together, and Weston was playful with her too."

Her smile may have been a product of the talking point, but he'd take it however he could get it. "Oh, yeah! Sprite is a sweetheart."

"I love Sprite!" Camille stepped up beside Lucas and stuck out a hand to Maddie. "I'm Camille, Noah's fiancée." She stuck a thumb over her shoulder to indicate the brother swinging Levi in a circle.

Maddie's smile didn't change. She held the fake one Lucas thought she'd reserved for only him. "It's good to meet you."

"Yeah, it's great to have another woman around here. Not that I could ever get lonely around this bunch." Camille playfully shoved Lucas's shoulder. "I hear you're a horse whisperer. Lucas was singing your praises earlier."

Lucas dramatically slapped a hand over his face. "Don't give away the farm! Let her sweat it a bit before her evaluation."

When Maddie's eyes grew wide, Lucas chuckled and winked at her. "I'm kidding. You're doing fine. After supper, we can head back over to the stables and you can let me know how things went today."

Maddie nodded and tucked her chin before looking anywhere except at him.

"All right. It's suppertime," Mama called, and everyone took their places in line.

Long picnic-style tables ran the length of the meeting room, and Lucas shoved food onto his plate in a rush to grab a seat close to Maddie. The seat on her left was already taken by Camille, but Lucas plopped down on her right side.

Everyone usually ate for a few minutes before casually talking through the rest of the meal. There was a reason they called it the meeting room instead of the dining room. They talked through their work load each morning, assigning tasks and scheduling important things first to make sure everything that needed doing could get done in a day. After meals, they checked off the things they'd completed and added things to the list for tomorrow.

Now would be the time to talk about how her first day went, but he'd asked her to come to the stables with him after supper because what they did seemed different from the other ranch tasks. Sure, Lucas worked the fields and tended the cattle like his brothers, but no one else cared for the horses. That part of the ranch felt like his responsibility, and no one else understood it.

But Maddie would understand it, and their unspoken link wasn't something he wanted to share.

CHAPTER 5
LUCAS

After the meal, Maddie offered to help clean up, but Mama Harding shooed her away before handpicking Micah and Hunter as her helpers.

"Come on." Lucas waved her toward the exit.

After an unsure glance over her shoulder, she followed him into the growing dark. The sun had barely set, and the sky was still starless.

"We can take my truck." Lucas pointed toward his blue pickup. "I'll bring you back." She'd already worked twelve hours today, and he didn't intend to keep her long.

Maddie glanced at her truck as if contemplating her options before silently climbing into his.

Trying not to scare her off, Lucas held his tongue. She hadn't responded to his natural talkative side. Maybe silence would make her comfortable until she was ready to talk.

They stepped into the stable where Vader and Blane were stalled on opposite ends. He'd installed dim lighting for the night, and he flipped them on hoping she'd be more at ease.

"Everything went well," Maddie said as she stepped up to Vader's stall. "I don't really have anything to report. They seem to be well maintained."

Lucas nodded. Every tool was in its place and the horses seemed content. "Great job. Did you enjoy it?"

Maddie looked his way for once, and he was met with a raised, questioning brow. "Did I enjoy what?"

"Your day. Do you like it here?"

The tension in her expression relaxed, and she leaned back against the wall. "I had a great day. I got to hang out with the horses all day. I think Dolly will like it here."

"She will. I hope you'll like it here too." Lucas stepped closer to her, still leaving a couple of feet between them. "We need someone like you."

"Like me?" Maddie questioned.

Her face held an innocent air. He wasn't sure if it was the braid or the porcelain tone to her skin, but her question held the hope of a child fishing for approval from a parent.

"We need *you*, actually. I can tell when someone

has a connection to the horses. It's something I feel every day, but I don't think there are many other people who understand it. I get the feeling you do."

Maddie swallowed hard, and his gaze was drawn to the slight curve of her exposed neck.

"I get it," she whispered, gaze finally locked on his.

Quietly, he asked, "Why didn't you say anything when I mentioned the snakes this morning?"

She tucked her chin and shrugged. "It wasn't important."

"Getting to know you is important to me. I was really young the last time you were here. I didn't know you were that girl who helped me find snakes."

Maddie's mouth lifted on one side. "I got in a lot of trouble too for putting snakes in people's boots." She hugged her middle and shifted her weight to her other foot. "The pranks were fun, but Mom and Dad hated them. They didn't want me to mess things up for them here."

Lucas took his hat off and hung it on the nearest stall door. "I'm sorry. I was just a kid, and I didn't know you got in trouble."

"It's water under the bridge. I just can't afford to goof off here. I need this job."

Lucas rubbed a hand over his face and through his hair. "I get it. I'm not like that anymore. I still have fun, but nothing involving snakes."

"Or mud?" she asked.

Lucas grinned, remembering one particularly muddy afternoon with her when they were kids. "Well, I still get muddy sometimes, but not on purpose."

Maddie's grin was small, but it was genuine this time. "Got it."

Lucas nodded toward the door with his chin. "Let's go check on Dolly before we go."

He grabbed his hat, and she stepped out of the stable before he turned off the lights and closed everything up.

Maddie patted the side of her leg, and Dolly trotted over to the fence. "Hey, girl."

Lucas made his way over and offered a hand to Dolly. He was closer to Maddie than he had been all day, and he could feel the heat from her body dissipating into the cool night around them.

Dolly pushed her face into Lucas's hand, and he nuzzled close to the newcomer.

"Hey, what about me?" Maddie scoffed. "You remember your mama?"

Lucas leaned closer to Maddie. "Don't take it personally. The ladies love me."

He barely saw her eyes roll in the dim moonlight, but her smile was bright. He couldn't look away.

"All the ladies?" she asked playfully.

Lucas shrugged. "It's a blessing and a curse."

She laughed, and it was the most beautiful sound he'd ever heard. His chest constricted at the joyful noise that was punctuated by a gasp for air that sent his pulse racing.

"I should get back." Maddie pointed toward the truck.

"Yeah, it's been a long day. I know these long hours are tough, so let me know if you need a break."

"I'm fine. I like being with the horses, and your mom said I can get a cabin here soon. I really appreciate everything."

So, Maddie was moving to the ranch. Lucas liked that idea. "I'll get started cleaning out your place soon. It shouldn't take me long." He'd need an evening chore to keep his thoughts off Maddie.

He dropped her off at her truck and watched her drive away. He'd learned more about her today than he expected after their rocky start this morning.

Deciding to get a head start on her place, he made his way toward the closest empty cabin to his own. It wasn't falling apart, but it would need quite a bit of work.

The wrangler's cabins were probably a hundred years old and built for men who spent little time indoors. Each had a small kitchen, living area, bathroom, and bedroom. The kitchens didn't get used very often since Mama cooked every day. There were two clothes washers and dryers at the main house, and Mama took care of all the laundry while the men worked the fields.

He made a mental note to thank his mama for everything she did for him and his brothers. She was like the mechanic of the ranch workers. She kept everyone fed, clothed, and ready to work.

Lucas hoped one day he'd end up with a hard-working woman like his mama. He hadn't put much stock in searching for someone to spend his life with. He was young and wanted to be worthy of a wife before he set out looking.

Maybe he wouldn't have to look far because Maddie was quickly flooding his thoughts.

Pushing the idea from his mind, Lucas pulled a notepad out of his back pocket and began writing the list of things he'd need to fix up the cabin for Maddie.

He'd be better when he was older, and, Lord willing, there'd be time to find a good wife later.

When it came to finding the woman he'd spend his life with, he decided to give it to the Lord.

CHAPTER 6

MADDIE

The next week, Maddie braided her hair over her shoulder as she got ready to head over to the ranch. The cool morning wind nipped at her sleeveless arms, and she decided to grab a long-sleeve shirt just in case it got cool again this evening. Her T-shirt that read *Whatever lassos your longhorn* would be sufficient for the heat of midday, but she'd been working till after dark most nights.

She was early for work today, so she whipped the truck into Sticky Sweet's Bakery on Main Street for a morning treat. She'd discovered the place last weekend, and their doughnuts were delicious.

Falling into line, she studied the menu to avoid having to make eye contact with anyone. She didn't know anyone here, and she wasn't sure she wanted to yet. The barista, a young girl named Victoria, had been excessively friendly to Maddie last time she stopped by.

It would be easy to make friends, but if her job at the ranch didn't work out and she had to leave—again—she knew it would be hard to break those ties. Continuously guarding her heart was exhausting.

The two men ahead of her ordered, and she stepped up to the counter.

Victoria's chipper tone was brighter than usual this morning. "What can I get you, sweetheart?"

"I'll just have a coffee and a doughnut, please."

"Coming right up," Victoria sang before rattling off the cost.

One of the men in a blue firefighter T-shirt stepped up to her. "Well, fancy meeting you here."

Maddie's attention bolted up to find Lucas standing in front of her. She stammered as if she were a kid caught with her hand in the cookie jar. "Uh, hey." She focused on handing Victoria the correct change.

"You headin' to the ranch?" Lucas asked.

She stepped to the side to allow the next person to order, but Lucas was standing very close to her in the crowded bakery, and she had no choice but to notice his hard-lined jaw.

"Yeah, I don't have to be at work until seven." Maddie tucked her elbows in and stroked her braid with one hand.

She tried not to meet Lucas's gaze, and there wasn't anywhere else to look except straight forward at his muscular chest. Tucking her chin, she tried to avoid him entirely, but it was impossible in the confined space.

"Can I catch a ride with you?" Lucas asked. "Noah wanted to run by Camille's place before she had to go to work, and I need to get home."

Maddie looked up at him. His question had drawn her attention, and she'd given in to the impulse. "Okay, sure."

He was a head taller than her, and standing this close, she could make out the slight crook in his nose. Somehow, she found the flaw endearing. His dark eyes were solely focused on her, as if the entire bakery had faded away.

Noah shoved Lucas's arm when his order was called before waving good-bye.

Lucas turned to accept his coffee from a disgruntled Victoria. Her mood had flipped in a hurry, and she narrowed her eyes at Maddie.

So much for the possibility of friends.

"Thanks, Victoria. Have a good day." Lucas raised his cardboard coffee cup to her, but she ignored him.

Unfazed by her dismissal, Lucas drew his attention back to Maddie. Once again, she felt like the world had stopped turning around her simply because she was caught up in his intense stare.

In her observation, he looked tired. She hadn't seen him in two days, and the family had filled her in that Noah and Lucas were also firefighters and their shift kept them from the ranch two days a week.

"So, you're here for the officer's special?" Lucas asked with a grin.

"The what?"

"Coffee and doughnuts."

"Oh, yes. Their doughnuts are wonderful, and I need the caffeine pick-up to get started in the morning."

Lucas lifted his cup. "I just need to make it back to the ranch without falling asleep."

Maddie tilted her head. "Tough shift?"

"You could say that." Lucas rubbed a hand down his face and gave a deep sigh. "There are times when two days at the fire station is harder than five days at the ranch. It might be easier if I got more sleep."

Victoria called Maddie's name, and she accepted the offered cup and bag without making eye contact with the barista. "Thanks."

"You ready?" Lucas asked.

Maddie nodded, and Lucas opened the door for her as they left the bakery. At the truck, he opened the driver's side door for her first before making his way to the other side. Even his walk seemed tired. He sank into the seat with a contented sigh and didn't even attempt to chat on the way to the ranch.

With his head rested back, his eyes drifted closed each time she stole a glance.

"Where do you want me to take you?" Maddie asked.

"My cabin would be great. I need a nap before I try to operate any heavy machinery today."

She'd seen the cabins running along the east side of the ranch and made her way toward them. "Which one is yours?"

"Third one down," Lucas answered without opening his eyes.

She parked the truck in front of his cabin. "Here you go."

"Thanks for the ride." Lucas pointed toward his right. "That one there is yours. It's not ready yet, but I'm working on it."

When had he had the time to work on her cabin? She'd been at the ranch less than a week, and he'd been gone two of those days.

"No rush. I'm fine at the hotel."

Lucas huffed, but a grin played on his lips. "Said no one ever."

"If you'll let me know what needs fixing, I'll do it myself," Maddie offered.

"I'll take care of it. Besides, I'm here later, and I can work on it at night." Lucas shrugged and opened the door.

"Good night, Maddie."

She couldn't fight her grin at the odd comment. "Night, Lucas."

Once he disappeared inside the cabin, she made her way to the main house for breakfast. She ate the doughnut in her truck before heading inside.

Noah wasn't at breakfast either, and she wondered how he and Lucas managed multiple jobs and responsibilities. From the look of Lucas this morning, he wasn't fit for much work today.

The family made a plan for the day's work, but it didn't really include her. There had been one day at the end of last week when they'd asked her to stable four of the horses at night so they'd be easy to saddle in the morning to move a herd. The change of pace had been a little exciting.

Just before lunchtime, Lucas strolled into the stable looking like a new man. His eyes were bright, and his step was quick.

"Morning, Maddie."

"Morning, Lucas. How was your nap?"

"Oh, I didn't get much of one. Micah called at about nine and needed a hand." He observed the horse Maddie was grooming intently before running a hand over her silky black side. "Morning, Sadie."

Maddie watched as the horse leaned toward Lucas. Sadie was a wild one, and Maddie had been caught off guard by her a number of times already.

Watching Lucas love a horse made Maddie's heart melt. Lots of people loved horses, but few had that special connection to them that she could see with Lucas.

Maddie had formed an unbreakable bond with horses in her early teen years when social interactions and friendships had been hardest for her to foster. It had taken years of therapy to overcome the deep-seated idea that if her parents hadn't loved her, no one could.

The two people in this world who were bonded to her by instinct and blood hadn't put her first, and that would always sting. They'd always had a hands-off approach to parenting, and she recalled aching for their attention and love at an early age.

So, Maddie understood Lucas's connection to the affectionate animals. She clung to the horses too. They loved her and wouldn't leave her.

Unlike her parents, Aunt Brenda had been the one person in her life who had loved her unconditionally. Her aunt had fought tooth and nail to gain quick guardianship of Maddie after her parents were incarcerated.

It was hard being away from Aunt Brenda now, but at least she had the horses to keep her company here. Watching Lucas, she admired him and the affection he showed Sadie.

He turned his attention to Maddie, still smiling from his nuzzling with the horse. "You like what you see?" he playfully asked.

Maddie smiled despite her better judgment. "I

was checking out your horse, but if your ego needs a boost, I can move my attention a little to the right."

Lucas's brown eyes held a gold tint in the dim stable lighting as he stepped closer to her.

She shouldn't have been so bold. He was her boss, and darn it, she knew better than to encourage him.

"I'd always appreciate your attention, Maddie. You sure have mine."

Her blood ran cold then hot in her veins, and she stood paralyzed as his intent gaze dared her to move. When she felt the heat in her cheeks, she broke the stare.

Lucas turned to walk away, yelling over his shoulder, "See you at lunch. And, Maddie…"

She lifted her head to see him standing in the stable doorway looking like a silhouette of a perfect cowboy.

"I like your shirt." He tipped his ivory cowboy hat to her and rounded the corner of the stable.

Yep, Maddie Faulkner was a goner if she didn't get a handle on her reactions to the charming Lucas Harding.

CHAPTER 7

MADDIE

Lucas was as animated as ever at lunch. He playfully shoved Aaron out of a seat next to her, and she felt like she was the object of a second-grade crush.

Being around the family was easy and hard at the same time. What a paradox. They laughed and picked on each other, but they also didn't pull punches. The dynamic was captivating to her wandering heart.

But sometimes, she wondered how she got the short end of the stick when it came to family. Sure, her Aunt Brenda was great, but her parents were the worst. If she'd grown up in a family like the Hardings or even spent more time here as a kid, she might not have turned out so messed up.

Lucas made several attempts to include her in the conversation at lunch, and supper was no different. Camille was present for the last meal of the day, and the topics were generally more lighthearted until it came time to talk shop.

So far, Maddie liked Camille. She seemed happy here at the ranch, and she lit up like a Christmas tree with Noah at her side.

Maddie looked away from the far side of the table where Noah and Camille sat, wrapped in each other's gazes. Would a man ever look at Maddie that way?

In her conscious effort to avoid Noah and Camille, Maddie noticed the dark-haired, tan-skinned cowboy at the other end of the table. She'd been reintroduced to Hunter, but she hadn't heard hide nor hair from him since.

She remembered Hunter from her last stay at Blackwater Ranch. He'd been a few years older than her, and his scowl hadn't been much more than a frown back then. What drew her eye now was the thick scar that ran from the outer corner of his eye to his jaw. She didn't want to know how he'd acquired the deformity.

Maddie stood with her empty plate and walked with Mama Harding toward the industrial-size trash can. "I'd like to help you clean up. You haven't let me yet."

Mama Harding's soft brown eyes reminded Maddie of Lucas's. What a blessing to have parents who shared their eye color as well as their love with their children.

"Oh, don't worry about it. Your day will come." Mama Harding nudged her shoulder against Maddie's.

Lucas stepped up behind his mother, wrapped her in a hug, and kissed her on the cheek. "Thanks for supper. Love you."

Mama Harding patted her son's arm. "Love you too. You think you could help me clean up this evening?"

Lucas's shoulders dramatically sank, and he feigned hurt. "Mama, I was hopin' to—" His gaze flashed to Maddie. "I just—"

"That's enough whining," Mama Harding softly chided. "Get to the kitchen. You can wash, and I'll dry."

Lucas gave Maddie a longing look as he replied, "Yes, Mama."

When his mother turned her back, Lucas whispered, "Stay with me?"

Maddie's stomach fluttered at his request. "I already offered to help. She turned me down."

"What?" Lucas whisper yelped. "That ain't right. The woman is on a power trip. Someone has to stop this madness."

Maddie giggled. The sound bubbled out of her without her consent, and it felt glorious.

With one last look into Lucas's pleading eyes,

she knew she needed some space. She'd had a wonderful day from the get-go. If she'd learned anything at all from her high school studies of the memorable *Romeo and Juliet*, it was that too much of a good thing was really a bad thing.

Maddie stuck her hands in the back pockets of her jeans. "I really need to get on back to the hotel."

Lucas brushed his fingertips against the outside of her hand. "One day, I'll teach you how to live a little." He strode off toward the kitchen where his mother waited for him.

Warmth still lingered where he'd touched her, and she was stunned by the novelty of the gesture. Pulling herself from a daze, she said her quick good-byes and stepped into the early night. After spending every daylight hour at the ranch for a week, she was beginning to long for the nights here too.

Thoughts like that were dangerous. She was getting attached. The mere idea had her chest aching. She was headed for disaster. No one had mentioned her parents yet, so she had to believe that the Hardings didn't know about what happened when she was a kid.

Surely, they knew. At least Silas and Anita anyway. One morning, both of Maddie's parents had held jobs at the ranch. By midnight, they'd been hushing her cries as they shoved her into a beat-up sedan and drove away.

Maddie turned up the radio to drown out the memories. She hadn't thought about her parents in a while. Tonight was too soon.

Stepping into her hotel room, she closed the door and let the silence settle around her. She leaned her back against the door and closed her eyes. She could do this. She'd survived everything up until now, and she was safe with the Hardings. Her parents weren't here to mess things up this time.

Maddie needed to clear her mind, and it'd been too long since she'd written in her journal. One especially helpful therapist—in the long line of professionals who her Aunt Brenda had hired to help Maddie overcome the emotional damage her parents had inflicted—suggested writing. Surprisingly, writing was the perfect therapy for Maddie. If it was on the page, she didn't have to say it out loud to feel the weight lift from her shoulders.

She showered and put on her most comfortable pajamas. Tonight, she needed all the comfort she could get.

She sat crisscross applesauce on her bed and opened her journal. The book was almost filled, and she made a note to tell Aunt Brenda she needed a new one. Maddie didn't mind buying her own journals, but her aunt enjoyed picking out inspirational ones for her. Her aunt always wrote encouraging words on the first page before giving it to Maddie.

With the journal open before her, she closed her

eyes and breathed. Her entries were prayers. Words meant for only her and her Savior. When she had trouble thinking of the words to pray, she wrote them instead.

Lord, I come to You today praying for peace. My mind is at war with my heart, and I just needed to talk to You. Her breaths came easier when she wrote and closed off her mind to anyone but the Lord.

Dear God, I don't know what comes next. I don't know if I'll get to keep this place—or these people—that I...

She paused, unable to write the words. She couldn't love them. They weren't her family to love. They were just being nice to her, but they weren't hers.

She choked on a sob before her pencil returned to the page. *God, I need You. Please help me to understand Your path for me. I want to follow it, but I don't know where to go or where it ends. I'm afraid. No, I'm terrified. Lucas said he wants to show me how to live a little, but what if he does? What if I live and I like living? What if I live too much and I go out in a flaming rush? Shakespeare said it, and he was right. Violent delights lead to violent ends.*

It's better if I just keep my distance. I don't know how much longer I can, but I don't know if I'll be strong enough to handle it if I have to leave the ranch again.

A tear dripped onto the page, and she dabbed at it with the bedsheet.

This is only temporary. It's not my home. I'll only have one home, and I won't see it on this earth.

None of this is real. This isn't my home, and this isn't my family.

Maddie stared at the words on the page as she wrote the last line.

If it's not real, it can't hurt me.

It was a lie. Her heart felt it. It was real, and that meant she'd need the strength to face the Hardings when they found out she was the daughter of thieves and sent her packing.

CHAPTER 8
LUCAS

Lucas headed toward the kitchen in a daze. The lack of sleep was causing his eyelids to feel heavy again.

His mother's gentle hand landed on his shoulder, and she took the dishes from his hands. "You go on, baby. I know you didn't get a break after your shift. I can handle this. I just wanted to make sure you were okay."

Lucas nodded. He'd wake up early in the morning and help her with breakfast.

She pulled him in for a quick hug. "How are things at the station?"

"Fine. We just had back-to-back calls all weekend." Lucas released their embrace and rubbed his eyes. "I need to hit the hay. I love you, Mom."

"Love you too."

Camille stepped into the kitchen and gave Lucas

a quizzical look. "How are you still upright? Noah crashed as soon as dinner was over."

"I'm not far behind him," Lucas confirmed.

"How's it going with Maddie?" Camille asked. "She still doesn't look completely comfortable at meals. Is it because of all the men, you think?"

Lucas shrugged. "I wish I knew. She seems perfectly happy around Asher."

Instinctually, his heart rate picked up. Why did it bother him so much that Maddie preferred his brother's company?

Camille leaned against the doorframe. "Well, hello, jealousy. Fancy meeting you here."

He was supposed to deny it, but if he was honest, the emotion boiling inside of him was jealousy.

"I've tried to be nice, but she just doesn't seem to like me. She mentioned earlier that I got her into some trouble when she was a kid—which I had no idea—so that could be it."

"Maybe she's trying to avoid that kind of distraction," Camille offered. "She takes her job seriously, and she probably wants to keep it."

"I'm not trying to get her in trouble. I like her here," Lucas said.

"You like her here, or you like *her*?"

Lucas cut his glance to the floor. "I don't know. I do like her. How could I not like her? She loves horses as much as me, but I haven't really talked to

Mom and Dad about their thoughts on dating another ranch worker."

Mama Harding slung the dishrag over her shoulder and leaned her hip against the counter. "It's fine by me and your father, but you need to make sure you're mature about it. Make sure it's what you really want because we're gonna expect you to continue working together if things fizzle out."

"That's fair," Lucas agreed.

Was this what he really wanted? He was certainly attracted to Maddie, and they shared a deep love of horses. She seemed kind and hardworking, and Mama had mentioned that Maddie had attended church with the family on Sunday while Lucas had been on his shift at the fire department. What else could they need to be compatible?

Pretty women were a dime a dozen in Blackwater and the surrounding cities, but Maddie seemed to shine brighter than anyone else he'd ever known. She wasn't flashy or showy; instead she was a subtle beauty. Was it her instinctual understanding and care for the horses that attracted him? Was it her guarded emotions and unspoken drive?

Lucas pondered his mother's advice. He liked Maddie, but she didn't seem to share the same interest in him. After all, he was still wondering if she had her eye on Asher.

Lucas's mother gave him a double tap on the

back. "Just take it to the Lord. If the two of you are meant for each other, then you'll figure it out. Now go on. Get some sleep." She kissed his cheek and swatted him with her dishrag.

"Night, Mama. Night, Millie."

Lucas made his way home in a tired fog, assured he would have a better day with Maddie tomorrow after a good night's sleep.

The next morning, Lucas arrived early to breakfast. The day after his shift at the fire station was the toughest, but he was ready to go once he got a long rest and reboot.

He wasn't the first to arrive at the main house. Asher's truck was parked out front. With the night's rest and a beautiful morning, Lucas's mind wasn't as clouded by jealousy for his brother. He'd taken his mom's advice and prayed about Maddie, asking the Lord to reveal what exactly that relationship was meant to be.

Lucas didn't have all the answers, but he felt more confident that he should just continue being kind and welcoming to her, and the rest would show itself in time.

For now, he decided he could find out more about Maddie from Asher. It wouldn't hurt to know what his brother knew.

Lucas walked in and hugged his mama. "Morning, sunshine."

"Morning, baby. How'd you sleep?"

"Like a rock."

Asher stepped out of the kitchen carrying a tray of biscuits.

Lucas pointed to his brother. "I need to talk to you."

"Whatever it is, I didn't do it," Asher qualified.

"I just wanted to talk about Maddie. She seems to like you."

Subtlety was for chickens. Lucas wanted to know if Asher was interested in Maddie and vice versa.

"She's a good woman. I remember her from back when her parents worked here. She was a little younger and surrounded by a bunch of rambunctious boys." Asher lifted a shoulder as if that were enough explanation. "She wanted to fit in and be included, but she wasn't always sure of herself. I didn't like seeing her left out, so I invited her along a lot. She needed that confidence boost."

Interesting. "So, what is she self-conscious about?" Lucas asked.

Asher turned to him and narrowed his eyes. "You don't know? You're so dense."

"What? I can't know if I don't know!"

Strong argument, Lucas.

Asher grinned, taunting Lucas. "I think she had a

crush on you... when we were kids. She chased after you and always hung around you with stars in her eyes. She never said anything directly, but it always bothered her when you didn't give her the time of day. She didn't care so much if the others didn't notice her."

Lucas tried to temper his reaction. "Are you serious? But what about—"

Asher held out his hands. "What about what?"

"Um, what about you? Do you... like her?"

Asher crossed his arms over his chest and gave Lucas a once-over. "What if I do?"

Lucas threw his hands in the air. "I don't know. Stop making this harder than it has to be. Just answer the question." Their brothers were slowly trickling into the meeting room, and Lucas didn't want to have this conversation in front of an audience.

Sometimes, it was hard to communicate with Asher. They were so much alike, and there were only a handful of things they took seriously between the two of them.

Asher tried to conceal his grin. "I'm just messing with you. I like her as a person, but I just don't think I'm the one for her. Plus, she hasn't ever given me any signs that she's interested in me either."

Lucas shoved his brother's shoulder. "Why didn't you just say so? You had me going."

"I won't lie. It was fun watching you sweat." Asher walked off, laughing at his own smarts.

Lucas went to join the rest of his brothers. Had Maddie really had a crush on him back then? The rational part of him said that crushes aren't mature feelings and they didn't mean anything after the age of ten. However, the ever-growing hopeful part of him wondered if an old crush could lay the ground-work for something more.

Noah nudged Lucas's arm and asked, "Where's Maddie this morning?"

Looking around, Lucas saw no sign of her. "I don't know." He checked his watch. Mom would be calling them to eat any minute now. "I'll see if she's at the stable."

Lucas stepped outside and craned his neck toward the stables. When he didn't see Maddie's truck parked out front or by the barn, he called her.

She answered quickly and spoke fast. "Hey, I'm so sorry. I'm on my way. I'm running late."

The fear in her voice sent a jolt of concern to his chest. "Easy, Maddie. I was just checking on you. Don't rush."

She huffed an exaggerated breath. "I'm so sorry. I'm never late. It's so unprofessional, and everyone is gonna think I'm a flake!"

Lucas laughed and hoped his relaxed attitude would put Maddie at ease. "Listen. Things happen, and we all know that. No one is perfect, and we give grace around here. Ease off the accelerator and get here when you can."

Maddie's voice shook when she spoke. "I'm so sorry, Lucas."

He picked at a splinter in the wooden wall next to the door. "Don't worry about it, Maddie. Just get here safe."

"Okay."

She'd sounded unsure, but Lucas hoped she took his words to heart. It would crush him if she had a wreck trying to rush to get to work on time.

Lucas walked back inside and laid a hand on his mother's shoulder. "Hey, I need to run an errand before I get started today. I'll catch up with Micah in a little bit for orders."

Mama Harding patted his hand and pointed toward the counter filled with food. "Grab a biscuit. Can't have my crew working on an empty stomach."

"I couldn't agree more." Lucas grabbed a biscuit and scooped a handful of bacon into a napkin before running out the door.

CHAPTER 9
MADDIE

Maddie didn't expect every day to be perfect, but this was one for the record books.

She'd overslept this morning after forgetting to set her alarm last night. When she'd gotten that natural adrenaline rush that came with being late, she'd poked herself in the eye putting her contacts in and danced around the bathroom with one hand over the wounded side.

After giving in and putting her glasses back on, she'd skipped a shower in favor of time and threw on a T-shirt with a cactus on it that read *Hard to handle*. Her evening shower was the important one anyway after brushing against the horses all day.

She slipped into her truck as the sun was coming up. There'd be no time to stop at Sticky Sweet's Bakery, and she probably wouldn't make it to breakfast at the ranch either.

Maddie steadied her trembling hands as the old truck rumbled to life. Even the worst bad days only lasted twenty-four hours. She could make it through this one, even if life kept throwing her curve balls.

Before the engine warmed up, Lucas called. She answered apologetically. He'd sounded understanding, but the call from her boss having to check up on her was almost too much this morning.

She was letting them down already. The Hardings had been good to her, and she was messing everything up. Tears pooled in her eyes, but she wiped each of them in turn before they had a chance to fall.

When she finally made it to Blackwater Ranch, she looked at the clock on the dash and realized breakfast was almost over. She decided to skip it altogether and drove straight to the stables.

The horses heard her coming and trotted to greet her at the fence. They were beginning a new morning ritual when she arrived.

The equines were lined up by the time she made it to the fence, and she nuzzled each of them. By the time she'd made it to Dolly's side, the other horses had moved on, satisfied with their morning attention.

"Hey, girl." Maddie closed her eyes and leaned in to her friend's neck. She needed this right now, just a moment with someone who cared. Breathing deep, she soaked in the morning air and hoped she could turn this day around.

The rumbling of a truck stole her peaceful moment, and she stepped away from Dolly. Technically, she wasn't late since she'd made it to the stable before her shift began. She just hadn't made it in time for breakfast as usual with the family.

It was Lucas, and someone might as well have dropped a brick in her stomach. He was her boss, and he didn't care about her bad morning. Setting her mind to work, she moved into the stable before his truck was parked.

As she'd expected, Lucas was hot on her heels, and she tried to ignore him as he entered the stable.

"Good morning," Lucas said behind her. "Is everything okay?"

Without turning to him, she nodded. "Of course. Why wouldn't it be?" Her voice was shaky, and she sucked in a shuddering breath to calm her nerves. He was her boss, not an executioner.

"You sounded frazzled on the phone. We don't punch a clock around here, so you don't have to worry about being late or anything. As long as the horses are cared for, everything is great."

Maddie nodded, afraid to trust her voice.

When she didn't reply, Lucas continued. "I brought you something."

Maddie's attention turned to him, sure that it was some tool or product for the horses.

Instead, he held out a white paper bag and a cup she recognized from Sticky Sweet's. His smile was bright in contrast to his blue shirt. The color suited him, and she decided blue was her favorite color.

"When you said you were running late, I was afraid you wouldn't stop for breakfast, so I got you something." He leaned in and whispered, "I also snuck one of Mama's biscuits and some bacon because protein is important."

Maddie didn't reach for the bag. She couldn't breathe. Every ounce of her energy was focused on holding the floodgates of her emotions.

He'd brought her breakfast because she was running late. No one besides her Aunt Brenda had ever done anything so thoughtful for her.

When she realized she wasn't going to win the battle with her emotions, she accepted the bag from him and opened it just to have a reason to look away from him. Bacon and a biscuit sat in the bottom beside her usual doughnut.

"Doughnuts and coffee," she stated.

"The officer special," Lucas confirmed with a genuine smile.

Maddie gathered the courage to look at him. "Thank you." The words seemed flat and meaningless, but they were all she had.

"You're welcome. I like seeing you get heart eyes over doughnuts." He waved a hand in front of his face. "The glasses look good on you."

Maddie smiled. She felt the tug on her lips and didn't wish to stop it. She was in a heap of trouble if he kept talking pretty to her and bringing her doughnuts.

Then, her traitorous chin began to tremble, and the tears came in earnest.

Maddie covered her face and sucked in uneven breaths.

"Whoa," Lucas said with hands up. "What's wrong?"

Maddie shook her head and wiped her eyes beneath her glasses, but the tears kept coming. "I'm sorry. I'm so sorry. I've just had a rough morning."

Lucas stepped closer to her and laid a hand on her arm. "I'm here. You want to talk about it?"

Maddie shook her head. "No, I'll be fine."

He opened his other arm to her, inviting her into his comforting embrace without demanding that she give him an explanation.

The temptation was too great, and she leaned in to his chest. His arms encircled her, and he didn't speak as she cried. She hardly ever cried anymore. She'd learned to handle rejection and disappointment early in life. How had one morning shaken her resolve?

As her sobs subsided, she reveled in the comfort Lucas gave. He was warm and strong and all around her. It was a side of him she hadn't seen before—a level of understanding she hadn't known to expect.

She held onto the feeling longer than was necessary, but everything about his embrace was new to her. Her parents had only provided what was necessary for her survival, and that didn't include hugs.

Now, she wanted to cry for a new reason. She was holding onto a man and her favorite food on a terrible morning. She'd eventually have to let him go, and everything about this moment had changed the way she felt about Lucas Harding. Knowing he could be fun *and* understanding was too much to fight against.

As his strong hand moved up and down her back in a soothing rhythm, she knew this closeness, this connection, felt too good to ignore. For the first time, she felt cared for by a person other than her aunt.

His soothing voice was low and calm. "You feeling better?"

Maddie nodded and forced herself to move away from him. "Yes. Thank you. I'm sorry I broke down like that." She brushed at her eyes. "It was really unprofessional."

Lucas laughed. "Yeah, we're really *professional* around here. You'll never fit in."

"You think you're funny." Maddie smiled as she ran a hand over her braid.

"I like to think so."

Her walls were cracking under the force of his

insistent friendship, and everything in her heart begged to move back into his embrace.

"Eat your breakfast. We have some important work to do today, and I could use your help."

Maddie sat on a nearby bench and pulled the bacon from the paper towel. "Sure, what are we doing?"

"It's my turn to check the herds, and I'd like for you to come."

Maddie looked around the stable. "But I'm supposed to take care of the horses."

"Yeah, but that doesn't take all day. I was thinking this is something we could do together."

He was including her, but she wasn't sure why. His insinuation that they would be doing something together drew up ideas of teamwork and camaraderie. The kindness he showed her had taken the sting out of her bad morning, and she found herself chewing fast, anticipating the rest of the day with Lucas.

After her hasty breakfast, they worked together to saddle Dolly and Sadie. He explained that Vader was his usual mount, but the stallion wouldn't get along with Dolly for their ride.

Was he always so thoughtful and understanding? It was too early to know.

Her position at the ranch was still new and uncertain, which reminded her that it would not be wise to get attached. As soon as Lucas found out what her parents did, he wouldn't waste any more time on her. He would probably ask his parents to fire her or just do it himself on the spot.

But as the day wore on and Lucas patiently pointed out what they were looking for as they checked the herds, any thoughts of protecting her heart were far from the beautiful day they shared riding their horses around the ranch.

By the time they tied up their horses at the main house for lunch, Maddie's bad morning was forgotten.

Lucas stepped around Sadie and met Maddie at the steps leading to the house. His smile was bright, and he reached out an open hand to her. She studied it as if the offering were a test before placing her hand in his.

The warmth flooded her hand and sent her heart beating wildly. She suddenly felt as if she could run for miles without tiring.

"Thank you for going with me," Lucas said. "It was great having someone to share the morning with."

The warmth had made its way to Maddie's chest. "Thanks for making my day better."

"Glad we could help each other. Maybe we could do that more often." He released her hand and tilted his head toward the door. "Let's go get something to eat."

They removed their boots at the door and hung

their hats on the rack. The smile hadn't left Maddie's face, and she said a silent prayer of thanks as she walked beside Lucas into the room.

Lord, thank you for growing days.

CHAPTER 10

MADDIE

Lucas began asking her to tag along on various projects and errands around the ranch. The change of scenery was nice, and many tasks included the horses.

One morning that week, he caught her as she was leaving breakfast.

"Hey, I was thinking we could get the horses squared away this morning and take a field trip to the feed and seed. I want your opinion on something."

Maddie had been too shocked to say yes and too excited to say no. Instead of answering, she nodded and grinned.

"Great. You want to just ride over to the stables with me, and we can take my truck into town?"

Maddie hopped into his truck and fed and groomed the horses. Lucas wanted *her* input about something to do with the horses for the ranch. Of course, he could choose not to accept her advice, but he'd asked for it as if he valued her opinion.

The horses were tended to faster than normal since she and Lucas were working together. Once she was in the truck, her excitement was impossible to contain. It would be a dream come true to one day be able to have a say in things, but she was still fairly new, and now was her time to prove her worth.

Lucas pointed out directions to the local feed and seed as he drove, and Maddie sat on the edge of her seat, paying close attention to road names and landmarks.

Blackwater wasn't far from Cody. In this part of the state, ranches separated the towns, and there wasn't much else in between. Still, Blackwater had a tiny stamp here, and she couldn't help but be charmed by the small town with its Old West feel and family-run businesses.

Lucas stopped in front of a large metal building and cut the engine. He pointed the tip of his truck key at the closest garage-style door. "This is Grady's. If you're looking for something for the horses, Grady will be able to help you find it."

Maddie logged the name away for later. She was treating this errand like a study session, and she was sure she'd be tested soon. These were the things she needed to know if she was going to stick around at the farm.

She followed Lucas into the store.

"Hey!" Lucas greeted a white-haired man wearing a pearl snap and slacks. "Maddie, meet my buddy, Grady. If you're looking for trouble, here's where you find it."

The man made a guffaw sound and slapped Lucas on the back. The smile on his face took the sting out of his words. "Boy, I know someone taught you to respect your elders."

Lucas laughed and laid a hand on the man's shoulder. "You're younger than me by a decade. You just don't use night cream like I do."

Grady shook his head as if Lucas were a lost cause. "So, you're Maddie? Lucas can't keep his trap from flapping about you every time he comes in here. It's good to finally put a face with a name."

He extended a hand for her to shake, and she accepted it on autopilot. Feeling the heat of a blush creeping up her face she said, "It's nice to meet you."

"The pleasure is mine. If you ever need supplies or someone to knock some sense into this one,"–he jerked a thumb toward Lucas— "I'm your man."

Grady's old eyes were kind and full of life. She loved him already. He had the look of a happy grandpa.

A fleeting thought crossed her mind. What had her own grandparents been like? Aunt Brenda's parents had died when Maddie was young, and she'd never met them as far as she knew.

"We'll catch up with you later, bud," Lucas said. "I just wanted to introduce you."

Grady waved him off and turned to Maddie. "He's strutting around here like a proud rooster because you're with him. I'd keep my eye on that one." He gave Lucas a conspiratorial look.

Maddie grinned. She loved the camaraderie between Lucas and the old man.

Lucas showed her around the store, pointing out items she may need on a regular basis. He'd said the ranch had a line of credit here, so she was welcome to stop by as needed.

When they reached the feed section, Lucas slipped his hand into hers and led her toward the selection. She was intensely aware of the heat where their hands touched, and she struggled to focus on his words. He pointed toward different supplements, but her attention was wrapped up in Lucas, just like her hand.

"What do you think? Should we put Weston on a high-calorie feed?" he asked at the end of his spiel. "He's much older than the others."

Maddie took a moment to process his words. In truth, Weston's ribs showed the tiniest bit.

"I'd say that's a good idea, but he doesn't need a high-protein diet, given the work he does."

Lucas rubbed his chin with his free hand and didn't release hers.

Did he even realize he was holding her hand?

She was having trouble thinking of anything else. Was holding hands with a woman so common to him that it could be overlooked?

She couldn't remember the last time she'd held hands with a man. In fact, the last person she'd been on a date with was Derek Simpson when she'd attended community college. He'd been barely eighteen and certainly not mature enough for a relationship.

Maddie tilted her head to observe Lucas as he continued pondering the choices beside her. Could it be true that Lucas was the first *man* she'd held hands with? If she was honest, she couldn't have picked a better man to be standing beside her. Her feelings for Lucas were growing every day, and if the way he sought her out was any indication, she thought he might like her too.

Lucas took her advice, and they chose a new feed to mix into Weston's diet. After they'd said their good-byes to Grady and loaded up the truck, he paused before getting in.

"You want to have lunch with me at Sticky Sweet's?" Lucas asked.

Maddie looked down the street toward the bakery. "Do they serve lunch? I've only been around for breakfast."

"Tracy makes the best peanut butter and jelly sandwiches."

Maddie laughed. "You have the palette of a toddler."

Lucas met her in front of the truck. "Levi doesn't seem to mind. We understand each other."

When she found herself too caught up in Lucas's stare to answer, he cleared his throat. "Is that a yes?"

"Oh, yes. Let's go."

Lucas grabbed her hand and squeezed. Would she ever get used to holding his hand or being the object of his affections? A flicker of fear told her to proceed with caution. She wasn't sure if he was a serial dater or a player. Those were things she didn't know too much about, considering her limited dating experience.

Sticky Sweet's was fewer than five blocks from where they were parked, but Lucas stopped and chatted with no less than a handful of people on the short walk. He always introduced her, but he gave each friend his undivided attention as he asked about family members by name and offered to check on ailing horses for neighbors.

Lucas never dropped her hand, but each person he spoke to held his eye contact and attention. He responded to every inquiry and closed the conversations with a promise to catch up soon.

Maddie marveled at the way Lucas made a friend everywhere he went. He made everyone feel special, and she suddenly felt that his friendliness to her may be a product of his personality instead of affection.

He'd caught her on a bad day earlier this week, and he probably thought she was mentally unstable after she cried at the sight of a doughnut.

Maddie was tired of the roller coaster of emotions she'd experienced since Lucas had become a part of her daily life. She'd never been able to open up and make friends or have a serious boyfriend, and the uncertainties were exhausting.

Lucas opened the door for her, and she entered the bakery ahead of him. When they reached the front of the line, he introduced her to Tracy before ordering two PB&J sandwiches.

"And anything Maddie wants."

She tilted her head and narrowed her eyes. "You don't have to buy my lunch."

Lucas placed a hand over his heart and dramatically said, "It would be my honor to provide you with a gourmet sandwich lunch."

Rolling her eyes, Maddie ordered a Reuben and joined Lucas at a table in the center of the room. She was getting used to the way he sought out the spotlight even as she avoided it.

Lucas leaned across the table with a smile. He only had eyes for her.

"You know, I'm starting to get used to this not talking thing."

Maddie grazed a hand down her braid. "What

do you mean?" They hadn't spoken much on the walk over, but there hadn't been silence. He'd greeted everyone he met.

"You just don't talk much, and it's something I'm getting used to. I think it means we have a super deep connection that doesn't need words. Like, we're past that."

Maddie laughed. "What?"

"Like a horse connection," Lucas explained.

Maddie shook her head, but her smile didn't falter. "No. Horse connections are between a person and a horse, not two people."

"But horse people understand each other, like how you understand me."

Lucas Harding confused her more than anyone she'd ever met, but her uncertainties probably arose from her budding feelings for him.

She whispered, "You think I understand you?"

Lucas shrugged. "You do. At least more than most. You don't roll your eyes at the things I say. You tell it like it is. You know what I would ask you to do for the horses before I say anything. You understand what's important to me because those things are important to you too."

It all made sense, but she couldn't gather the breath to agree with him. They did value the same things—God, the ranch, and the horses.

Except Lucas had a family—something she craved.

Tracy called their number, and Lucas jumped up to grab their order. Maddie didn't move while he was gone. She was still processing his idea that they had a horse connection. It sounded silly, but she knew what he meant.

Lucas set her sandwich and drink in front of her and laid his hand open on the table between them. "Mind if I say grace?"

Maddie placed her hand in his before bowing her head and closing her eyes.

Lucas's usual upbeat tone was reverent as he prayed. "Lord, thank you for this food and for sending Maddie to us when we needed her. Amen."

Shocked, Maddie opened her eyes to see Lucas digging into his sandwich. Had the Hardings needed her? His words made her sound so important.

She focused on controlling her emotions and watched him chew large bites of his lunch. A lump formed in her throat as she realized Lucas had the right mindset. She *was* important, just maybe not in the ways she'd experienced growing up. Jesus sure thought she was important, and she needed to remember that.

Taking a deep breath, she swallowed the first bite of her sandwich and ate with Lucas in the silence that didn't need words.

CHAPTER 11
LUCAS

Spending the morning with Maddie had been easy. It was almost too easy, and a few hours away with her felt like a vacation. He drove back to the ranch with Maddie at his side, feeling refreshed and ready to work.

The dry dirt billowed around his truck in a dusty fog as he drove past the main house to the stables. They unloaded the supplies they'd purchased, and Lucas dusted his hands on the front of his worn jeans.

"I'll be back in a few hours, but you can call me if you need me. I won't be far."

Maddie nodded, and the smile she'd worn most of the day had his blood pumping hard in his veins as she said, "Duty calls."

Lucas leaned against the nearest stall door, reluctant to leave her. "I have some super important work to do today. I'd ask you to come with me, but it's a surprise."

He was almost finished fixing up her cabin and couldn't wait to see her reaction. He didn't like the idea of her staying in a hotel, and she'd be more comfortable closer to Dolly.

"Oh, what kind of surprise?" she asked.

"Don't even try to pry it out of me. My lips are sealed like Fort Knox."

She chuckled and rolled her eyes. The mask she'd worn when she arrived here a few weeks ago was gone, but she still hadn't revealed anything meaningful about herself.

With an air of confidence he hadn't seen before, she placed her hands on her hips and shifted her weight to one side. The words *Loretta is my home girl* were bold and bright across her shirt.

"Fine, I'll just hang out with the horses while you're gone. By the time you get back, they'll have adopted me as their new mommy."

Lucas threw his head back. "Now I'm jealous." Of her for getting to hang out with the horses all day and of the horses for getting to spend the day with Maddie.

He turned his attention back to her and hesitated. The urge to tell her how he felt about her bubbled up in his throat, itching to be released.

"What? Why are you looking at me like that?" she asked.

"I really like hanging out with you," he confessed. "You don't think it's weird that I would rather hang out with the horses than most people."

The corner of her lips stretched to one side. "Horse people are different," she explained.

Lucas's eyes widened. "Yes! You know what it's like when you're dating someone who doesn't understand the whole horse thing, and they're always complaining because you spend too much time in the stables? Well, you don't do that."

It was true. He was trying to get comfortable waiting for her to tell him something about herself without pushing. Patience wasn't his strong suit, but he was old enough to know that working on himself was a good thing.

Maddie raised an eyebrow. "Did you just talk about me like I was one of your girlfriends?"

Lucas shook his head. When would she stop looking for the bad? "You say it like I have multiple girlfriends. I don't even have one."

"You could have a girlfriend." Maddie paused and looked away as if she were suddenly embarrassed. "If you wanted one."

He hoped she was right, but he only wanted one. Her.

"I don't see women lining up."

She tucked her chin, and he knew he'd pushed her out of her comfort zone.

One day, he'd convince her to hold her head high through everything.

One day, he'd tell her about his feelings for her, but she didn't seem ready today.

Lucas straightened his cowboy hat. "I just don't think a relationship would work out with someone who didn't understand why the horses are important. They're like people, and I don't want to be made to choose."

Maddie nodded. "I couldn't see myself dating someone who didn't understand them either. Granted, it's hard to meet someone when I'm here all the time."

Lucas's mood fell. Was she looking? For someone outside of the ranch?

Maybe he didn't have a shot after all.

Still, he didn't see a good reason to give up just yet. He still had work to do—on her cabin and her heart.

Lucas met Maddie in front of the main house for supper. She jumped out of her truck and burst into a laugh. "What happened to you?"

Lucas held his smile. He was covered in dirt, but he couldn't find the need to care.

"I've been working on your surprise," he explained.

"In the trenches?"

Lucas directed his attention to the dirt path leading to her new place. He hadn't been working in the trenches, but he had spent most of the afternoon in the primitive crawl space of Maddie's future cabin. It was hot and dry, but he'd finished leveling the flooring like he'd planned.

"Maybe. It's just dirt."

"But you look like you just snuck into the cookie jar. What's with the grin?"

He wanted to reach for her hand, but he wasn't sure how much he should push her. She'd let him hold her hand earlier, but he wanted to give her space.

"I'm just excited."

Lucas's smile fell when he noticed a familiar truck parked around the side of the house. Jameson Ford worked part-time at Blackwater ranch and sometimes more often during hay and calving seasons. He'd been focusing on his other part-time job at Chambers Dude Ranch since Maddie came to town, and Lucas had been lucky to avoid Jameson since.

There wasn't any true bad blood between Jameson and Lucas. They just didn't get along. Jameson was a hard worker, and he wouldn't know fun if it hit him in the face. He looked down on Lucas because he liked to joke around, but he always got his work done and then some. There was a silent competition between them to see who could work the hardest.

The urge to grab Maddie's hand grew stronger as they walked toward the house. He wanted a lifeline stretching between them so that Jameson wouldn't rattle the fragile relationship Lucas was building.

Maddie and Lucas left their boots at the door and their hats on the rack before joining half the crew in the meeting room. Jameson noticed Maddie immediately, and Lucas tried not to grimace.

Jameson was the same age and height as Lucas, but his build was thicker. Jameson kept a light beard between shifts at the fire station, while Lucas was clean shaven—most of the time.

Making a beeline for Maddie, Jameson focused all of his attention toward the beautiful blonde.

"You must be Maddie," he said, extending his hand. "Anita was just telling me about you. I'm Jameson Ford."

"Maddie Faulkner," she said as she accepted his hand. "I'm working with the horses."

"It's a pleasure to meet you," Jameson said. "I feel like I have some catching up to do since everyone else has known you for weeks. Will you sit by me tonight?"

Lucas wanted to throttle Jameson. What was with the crazy possessiveness? Lucas wasn't the jealous type, but he'd never vied with Jameson for a woman's attention before. Their competitive streak usually stuck to ranch work and sports.

Holding his tongue was tougher than he thought, but Mama Harding would paint his back porch red if he made a scene at the table. Instead, Lucas sat quietly on Maddie's other side at supper. His heart beat like the pounding of horse hooves against the dirt.

Seeing her talking and laughing with Jameson lit a fire in Lucas, and it was a destructive one. He wasn't showing Maddie his best side as he sat tense and silent beside her while Jameson asked her introductory questions she skirted at every turn.

After supper, Lucas hurriedly made his way outside, eager to fill his lungs with fresh air and focus on something besides Maddie and the confusion he felt when she was around.

Before he made it to his truck, the door opened again behind him, releasing the swirl of life and chatter from the meeting room into the warm night air before closing again.

"Lucas," Maddie called from behind him as she jogged from the porch to meet him.

He turned, full of excitement but afraid to hope. "Is everything all right?"

Her steps bounced as she stopped herself closer to him. "You left in a hurry. I just wanted to check on you."

He'd felt lost and hopeless before, but now, he

couldn't remember why. Maddie was here telling him—showing him—that she cared.

"I just wanted to get a head start on work for tomorrow." It was a partial truth. He was on his way back to her cabin to work for a few more hours.

Maddie narrowed her eyes at him. "It's kinda late to be working."

Lucas inhaled a deep breath. "I don't sleep much." He had too much energy to stay in a bed for more than four or five hours a night. His days usually started before the chickens and ended long after the rest of the ranch was asleep.

Maddie pointed over her shoulder at the main house. "You didn't look too comfortable at dinner tonight. Was it Jameson?"

Lucas hung his head. "Yeah. He's not a bad guy. We're just not..."

"It's okay. You don't have to tell me. I'm still getting to know people around here, and I just wanted to know if there was a reason he made you so uncomfortable." Maddie's shoulders rose to her ears, and she tucked her hands in the back pockets of her jeans.

"It's nothing to worry about. Like I said, he's a nice guy, just not my biggest fan."

Just then, Noah stepped out into the darkening night and lifted his chin to his brother. "You ready to get started? We can ride over together."

Lucas said, "Sure," before turning back to

Maddie. "We'll talk more in the morning. See you at breakfast."

"Yeah. See you soon." She stepped back toward her truck and started the engine.

Lucas waited until she'd pulled out before starting his own truck. Noah sat silent in the passenger seat.

"Thanks for helping me with this," Lucas said.

"No problem. You'll be helping me soon." Noah huffed. "You work the longest hours around here. We get a lot done at night."

Noah was building a house on the ranch for him and Camille to move into after they were married. Lucas didn't know much about their wedding plans. He just assumed they'd let him know when to show up and smile for photos. Until then, he'd be helping Noah with the building after ranching hours.

"That's the truth. I hadn't realized this cabin needed so much work. Thanks for making it a rush job."

Noah leaned against the truck door. "I know you want Maddie close. I think we all get it."

Lucas's brow furrowed as he drove over a bump in the road. "What are you talking about?"

"Well, you like her, don't you?" Noah asked.

"Yeah, but I didn't know everyone knew." Lucas sighed. "I don't want to scare her off, but I *do* like her."

"You'll figure it out. I mean, I don't know about her, but you don't have much dating experience."

Lucas scoffed at his brother.

"The kind of dating you do doesn't count. I mean relationship experience," Noah clarified. "Everyone needs time to learn how to be a part of a set. You've lived twenty-two years of your life on your own. A relationship means you have to think about someone else too."

Was Lucas doing that? He liked to think he was. He thought about Maddie a lot, and he worried about her more than he liked. Hopefully, that would change once he knew more about her. It was the things he didn't know that caused him the most anxiety.

"You're right," Lucas said as he parked the truck in front of Maddie's cabin. "It's not like it was easy for you to date Camille, and you'd known her most of your life."

Noah stepped out of the truck and sighed. "Yeah, I was a wreck through most of it, but it was all because I cared. She was worth it, and I would take that stress again any day for her."

That was the way Lucas felt about Maddie. She worked here now, and she wasn't going anywhere. He had time to get to know her. He'd just keep praying that the windows and doors to her heart would open.

CHAPTER 12
MADDIE

Maddie smiled despite the smell as she mucked out the stalls the next morning. The tension between Jameson and Lucas had been minimal at breakfast, even though Jameson had sat by her again.

Her job at Blackwater Ranch was turning out to be better than she'd expected. She just needed to keep her distance from any drama, and that included the Jameson-Lucas squabble.

She loved the horses, and they were all warming up to her. Dolly was happy here, and that eased some of Maddie's burden. She'd had to board her at a barn in Tennessee before, and she preferred being closer. Soon, she might even be living on the ranch. It had only been a few weeks, but she was beginning to feel at home.

Maddie shoved the pitchfork into the hay and

manure. Was it okay to like it here? She still wasn't sure how comfortable was too comfortable, and she caught herself floundering between contentment and reluctance to settle.

A few weeks wasn't enough time to know if her parents' mistakes would come back to haunt her. There was a chance she could mess up and get fired, but she'd try her best to make sure that didn't happen.

Her time at the ranch was ultimately up to the Hardings. If Maddie had her way, she'd settle into one of those wrangler cabins that lined the far side of the ranch and live out her days on this dirt.

Her chest constricted, and the breath she'd been inhaling stopped short. Daydreaming about a future here was sure to lead to heartache. Making a point to focus on the here and now instead of some silly fantasy, she wiped sweat from her cheek with the sleeve of her shirt and rested the pitchfork against the wall.

A few minutes later, Lucas stormed in wearing the same smile from breakfast. "Hey! You think we can finish up around here before lunch?"

Maddie scoffed and leaned on the pitch fork. "Work in the stable is never done."

Lucas let his head fall back and sighed. "I mean, whatever you're doing right now. We'll be back, but I wanted to have time to show you your surprise before lunch."

Maddie smiled and took a moment to appreciate his excitement. How many people would be giddy and bouncing on their feet to present a surprise to someone else? Lucas's heart was made for giving, and Maddie found herself lucky enough to be on the receiving end of his kindness.

"Sure. I'm just mucking out, so I'll stink. I hope we don't have to go anywhere nice."

Lucas waved his hand and grabbed the wheelbarrow handles. "Nah. We're not leaving the ranch."

Eager to find out about the surprise, Maddie worked double time with Lucas right beside her. Together, they finished in record time and washed up in the small shower room in the stable.

She followed him out to the truck and hopped in beside him. He drove toward the main house but continued on past it.

Jameson's truck was parked at the house as they drove by, and questions from the night before scraped at Maddie's mind.

"What's the deal with you and Jameson?" she asked.

When he didn't answer right away, she felt the heat rushing to her cheeks. She was getting too comfortable with him, and she'd crossed some unseen line.

"I'm sorry. I don't have any right to ask you about personal things," she amended. "Just forget I said anything."

"No, it's okay," Lucas said as he reached for her hand. Wrapping his fingers around hers, he continued. "Jameson and I are just different. That's all. There's no big secret. I'm just more of a fun-loving guy, and he's a stick in the mud."

Maddie bit her lips between her teeth to hide her obvious smile.

"We've always competed. In school, it was grades and sports. When we ended up in the same crew at the fire station, I thought it was a cruel joke." He turned to her with a smile. "We don't work well together. Micah usually sends us to opposite sides of the ranch." He turned his attention back to the path ahead.

Maddie could easily imagine the man she'd met last night being a worthy antithesis to the playful Lucas. She'd definitely sensed some jealousy after she'd given Jameson an iota of her attention, and she'd immediately felt guilty about it after Lucas had spent the morning focusing his affections on her.

"Now, he's always trying to one-up me on the ranch. I appreciate his hard work, but he won't miss a chance to throw it in my face." Lucas turned to her. "I'm talking too much, aren't I?"

"No, I'm just taking it all in," Maddie said.

"I'm the youngest around here, so by the time I was old enough to understand that everyone had to do their part and work the ranch, my brothers were already seasoned workers. I was the baby, always lagging behind. I tried my best and never left a job unfinished, but I guess I needed to prove my worth more than the others. I saw the pride in my dad's eyes when he looked at my brothers, and I wanted that. I wanted to be loved for more than being the baby."

"Lucas, I have *never* gotten the impression that your parents see you as the baby."

He grinned. "No, and you won't. Mom and Dad are pretty good about not playing favorites. I just always *felt* like the baby."

"You know, you technically *are* the baby of the bunch."

"Get out of here!" Lucas shouted with a huge smile. "I don't need your rational analysis. I'm just saying that by the time Jameson was hired, I couldn't help but think he was someone else I had to outwork to gain that respect from my parents. They deserve a hardworking son, and I want to be that for them."

Maddie looked down at their clasped hands in her lap. Lucas's hand was worn and rough, but hers wasn't exactly delicate and smooth. She wasn't a stranger to hard work, and she understood his struggle to feel worthy of his parents' pride. It was something she'd always wanted too, but her chance was gone now with her parents incarcerated.

"Thank you for telling me. I know I have no right

to ask you to share things about yourself since I'm kind of private."

Lucas lifted one side of his mouth in a heart-stopping grin. "I hadn't noticed."

Maddie shoved his shoulder and released his hand as they stopped in front of the wranglers' cabins. "Is my cabin ready?" she asked excitedly.

"Pretty much. Come on."

He met her in front of the truck and grabbed her hand again. The boards of the porch were new, as well as the columns.

"I can add a railing here if you want."

She let her fingertips trail along the smooth wooden column. "No, it's perfect."

At the front door, he entered first and turned on the lights before stepping back outside. "Go on," he said, motioning Maddie inside the cozy cabin.

The main room was open and spacious for the size of the place. The small kitchen to her left had been updated with new countertops, appliances, and a breakfast table. The other side of the open area was a living room with a couch and coffee table.

Lucas's shoulder brushed against hers. "Sorry, there isn't a TV. Only the main house has TV and internet."

Maddie placed a hand over her heart and turned to him. "What will I do without modern technology?"

Lucas shrugged. "I didn't know how you'd react

to any of this. I know it's small, but I can build onto it. Just let me know what you need."

"No way. I would never ask you to build onto my *free* housing. This is just fine." Truly, it was. The only part of her life that required lots of space was Dolly.

"Let me show you the rest." Lucas tugged her hand toward one of two doors. "Here's the bedroom, even though there's not much to see."

The room was large enough to hold the bed and a dresser. The mattress was bare, and the small window in the room was wide open. She made a note to buy bedding and curtains the next time she was in town. The thrill of decorating her own space grew as she made a mental list of things to do.

"The closet is average, but like I said, I don't mind building on if you need more space. It wouldn't be hard, but I'd need to get the walls up before we see snow."

Still holding his hand, she turned. Lucas was standing right behind her. His chest was close enough that she could feel the heat of his body.

Maddie stilled as every instinct told her to move into the warmth of his embrace. She hadn't forgotten the way he'd comforted her on her notorious bad day, and she wanted to feel his arms around her again. He'd given her the beginnings of a home, and appreciation hummed within her.

His expression was serious, and his intense gaze slipped from her eyes to her lips.

Was he going to kiss her? She was sure that she'd never wanted a man to kiss her more than in this moment, but the thought of actually kissing Lucas scared her to death.

His chest, so strong and incredibly close, rose and fell with the deep breaths that had his nostrils flaring slightly.

The sound of the silence in the cabin blanketed them until the walls faded away. It was just the two of them in a world that had come to a halt.

"Do you like it?" he whispered.

Lucas had done this for her. He'd made this old cabin livable for her all while working long hours in the field and at the fire station. He'd made a point to do something selfless for her above all else.

"I love it. It's perfect. Thank you," she whispered back.

With her head tilted up to him, their lips were only inches apart, and she thought her heart would explode in her chest from the anticipation.

A buzzing noise pierced the moment, and Maddie jerked.

"Ignore it," Lucas said.

It was his phone.

"You should answer that." Her breaths were deep and labored as she tried to calm her racing heart.

"It's not important."

"How do you know?"

Lucas lifted the hand he'd been holding and erased the space she'd put between them in her shock. Moving his fingertips delicately over the sensitive skin on the back of her hand, he traced a mesmerizing line that tingled in its wake.

"It's not more important than this—being with you."

If he said one more thing, she would break and kiss him. Gently pulling her hand from his, she cleared her throat and said, "Maybe we should get back. One of your brothers might be looking for you."

Lucas's gaze didn't falter as he studied her with a gentle expression. "Sure, let's go."

The phone call had startled her, and she'd panicked. She'd wanted him to kiss her, but the fear of *actually* kissing Lucas Harding had been too stressful to enjoy.

As they stepped outside into the beautiful midday sun, she hoped she hadn't discouraged him from trying to kiss her again.

CHAPTER 13

LUCAS

Maddie set the last box in the living room of her new cabin. "I guess that's it."

Lucas stretched his arms over his head. "Are you sure?" If they were finished moving her things from the hotel, everything she'd brought fit into four boxes that stacked neatly against the front wall of the tiny cattleman's cabin.

"Yep. I don't have much."

As happy as he was to find that the moving job wouldn't take more than one Saturday, a gnawing thought pestered him as he helped her unpack the boxes. Had she not brought a lot of things because she wasn't planning to stay?

He shook the negative thoughts from his mind as he unpacked a box of kitchen utensils. Maybe she just lived a minimalist lifestyle. It would be ideal for ranch living, since they didn't have ready access to a lot of modern conveniences like TV and internet. It wasn't as if she'd brought a box of movies and Xbox games.

"Where do you want these?" Lucas asked as he pulled the last piece of cookware from a box.

Maddie shifted her weight to one side and propped a hand on one hip. "I'm not sure."

"You want to come see my place? It might help you decide where you'd like to store some of this."

Maddie grinned and tilted her chin up. "That sounds like a great idea."

The sun was beginning to sink below the trees as they stepped from her porch. With her hand in his, they walked through the tall grass to his cabin nearby.

"Now, don't judge. It's a little messy. I didn't know anyone was coming over."

Maddie rolled her eyes. "I'm sure it's fine."

They stepped inside, and Maddie's jaw dropped. It was the reaction he'd hoped for.

"What is this?" She squealed. "It looks like one of those tiny homes on HGTV."

Lucas frowned. "What are you talking about?"

"You know. The home renovation channel."

"I don't have a TV!" Lucas playfully reminded her.

She laughed, and he wanted that sound in his cabin all the time. "Let's just say I'm impressed."

Lucas looked around at the wooden walls he'd

painted a rustic white, the mantle with horse sculptures lined atop it, and the hazy sconces that lit the room at intervals. "I fix things up when I can't sleep."

Maddie gasped. "Your kitchen is beautiful!" She moved through the small room and dragged her fingertips along the countertops.

A chill ran up Lucas's back as he imagined her fingers grazing the skin of his arm instead. He cleared his throat and started opening cabinets. "This is where I keep my pots and pans. Not that I use them that much. If I don't eat at the main house, I make a peanut butter and jelly sandwich to take with me."

Maddie laughed and stepped beside him to see the contents of the cabinet. "I like that layout. Does my cabin have those shelves?"

Her arm reached in front of him as she pointed, and he breathed in the smell of cinnamon and cedar wood. It was a smell that reminded him of a warm, comforting home.

"Um, no, but I can easily put some in for you."

Maddie leaned away from him and walked around the rest of the open space. "I love your cabin."

"It's nice enough for me. I don't spend a lot of time here. I pretty much just sleep."

Maddie let her gaze fall to the floor as she touched the back of the couch. "I've never spent enough time in one place to really make it my own."

"Is that why you didn't bring a lot of stuff?" Lucas asked.

She lifted one shoulder and let it fall. "I've never been attached to a place. All I need is a roof over my head and a place to hang my hat. I'm lucky to have that."

He stepped over to the couch and sat down before patting the spot beside him. "Where do you see yourself hanging your hat in a few years?"

Maddie's expression was shrouded in sadness as she sat. "There's no way to know that. I can't predict any of the future, much less years from now."

"I hope it's here," Lucas said.

Maddie turned to him, and the crease between her brows had only deepened.

"I hope you're here with me. I hope that's not too selfish, but I'm telling you the truth."

When she tucked her bottom lip beneath her teeth, he turned to face her. "You can have more than a temporary home here. There are people here worth getting to know."

Maddie whispered, "I know."

In a brave moment, Lucas leaned in and pressed his lips to her forehead. "I hope you stay, Maddie."

The warmth from his lips lingered, and she grinned. He had a way of making a forehead kiss seem deeply intimate. What would a true kiss feel like? The thought had warmth creeping up her cheeks. "I want to."

She looked at her watch and exclaimed, "Oh! I need to get back. I'm supposed to be meeting Camille for dinner tonight."

"Speaking of people worth getting to know. Camille is a good one."

Maddie stood and Lucas followed. "I know. I really like her."

"Where are you two going?"

"Barn Sour. She said they have the best totchos." Maddie laughed. "I didn't ask what totchos were."

"Oh, you are in for a treat. Totchos are my favorite. Can I come?"

Maddie ran a hand down her braid. "I think it's a girl's night."

"Well, can I have my own special night with you?"

"Like a date?" Maddie asked.

"Yeah. A date."

Maddie hugged her arms around her middle and smiled. "Yeah. I'd like that."

"Great. Now I feel better. Let's get you home."

Maddie stepped out into the new dark and laughed. "You have Christmas lights on your cabin?"

"Uh, yeah. They're pretty, and they make me happy."

"They do add some color to the place. I like them too."

Lucas grabbed her hand and started walking toward her cabin. "I can put some on your cabin too, if you want."

She laughed. "Are you serious? I actually think that would be cool."

"My lady gets what she wants."

Maddie stopped. "Your lady?"

"Well, not in a barbaric possessive way, but like, in a *I like you* way."

Maddie chuckled and began walking again. "I don't think I'll ever be bored here."

"All the more reason to stay."

CHAPTER 14
MADDIE

After spending more time at Lucas's house than she'd intended, Maddie threw on a light dress and fixed her braid before Camille was knocking on the door.

"I'm coming." Maddie grabbed her small brown purse and ran out the door.

Camille greeted her with a shocked expression. "Wow. You look amazing!"

Maddie closed the door behind her. "You saw me in a dress at church."

"But this one is adorable. I love the crossed straps in the back."

"Thanks. Are we taking your car?"

"Hop in," Camille said. "When do I get to see your new place?"

"Oh, you don't want to see it now. I just moved in today."

Camille jumped in and started the 4Runner. "Did Lucas help you?" Camille teased.

"He did," Maddie admitted sheepishly.

"How is that going?"

"What?" Maddie feigned ignorance.

"Oh come on," Camille begged. "I see y'all making heart eyes at each other all the time. He likes you."

Maddie swallowed hard, afraid to believe her friend's revelation. She knew Lucas liked her, and she knew her feelings for him were growing every day. The thing that terrified her was that she didn't know when it would end. Her feelings—and his—were bound to be casualties of life's unfair circumstances. She hadn't known anything different.

Desperate to change the subject, Maddie asked, "How's the house coming along? Lucas said you're building a house with Noah on the ranch, but I haven't been by to see it yet."

Camille sat up straighter. "It's amazing. I can't believe I'm going to be living here." Her voice took on a whimsical air as they turned onto the main road, leaving the ranch behind them. "I love this place."

The words almost burst from Maddie's mouth. *Me too.* But to say it would make it true. She couldn't afford to love this place. Giving her heart away was dangerous.

"When is the wedding?" Maddie asked.

"Probably next summer," Camille admitted. "We don't have a firm date yet."

They talked about the wedding until they pulled into the gravel parking lot at Barn Sour. Maddie could get used to Saturday nights like this, hanging out with Camille. She could get used to everything in Blackwater, including Lucas and his ridiculously beautiful eyes and thoughtful gestures.

Barn Sour was a casual local hangout with live music and a basic homestyle menu. The name's meaning wasn't lost on Maddie. Horses were considered barn sour if they were reluctant to leave the comfort of their barn or home. The music was well underway, and patrons danced through the open dance floor with delight.

She caught sight of the guitarist on the slightly raised stage and gasped. "That's Asher!"

Camille's laugh was barely audible over the music. "Yeah, he plays here with Hunter sometimes."

Maddie hadn't heard them play before, but their music was captivating. They sounded like professionals up on the makeshift stage.

"You wanna dance?" Camille asked. "I'll single lady dance with you if you want."

Maddie laughed, and the feeling was freeing. "I'm okay. Maybe later."

They settled into a booth on the wall opposite the stage and ordered drinks and totchos.

"I'm not gonna lie, I'm here for the totchos," Camille confessed. Her gaze cut to the entrance, and a pink tint covered her high cheekbones. She leaned over the table and pretended to whisper to Maddie. "I might also be here for the eye candy."

"What?" Maddie spat as she turned to follow Camille's line of sight. Noah was making his way through the crowd with Lucas beside him.

Maddie's heart rate kicked into overdrive. The band, the lights, the handsome cowboy. Her adrenaline was running wild. "I told him it was a girl's night. I swear."

Camille waved her off as the waitress set their drinks and totchos on the table. "Relax. I knew they would be here. They always try to show up when Asher and Hunter play."

Noah slid into another booth, but Lucas kept walking toward them until his brother grabbed his arm, pulling him back into the seat across from him like a rag doll.

Maddie shook her head and turned back to face Camille. "Those two are a mess."

"Agreed!" Camille popped a hot tater tot covered in cheese into her mouth. "These are so good and so bad."

Maddie picked a jalapeno off a nearby tot before trying it for herself. "It is good," she said around the mouthful of cheesy deliciousness.

Cheese stuck to her chin at the moment Lucas appeared at their table.

He rested the knuckles of his fists on the table and leaned in. "You must be a good thief."

Maddie froze. How did he find out about her parents? Bile rose in her throat, and she turned to Camille, hoping she didn't blow tater tot chunks.

"Because you stole my heart from across the room," Lucas continued.

She couldn't swallow the hunk of fried potatoes in her mouth, and a cold sweat broke out on her entire body. It was just a pick-up line, but her nervous system hadn't gotten the memo.

Camille swatted Lucas's arm. "Let us at least finish eating. Shoo."

"I'll be back." Lucas winked before dodging Camille's second slap and heading back to his table with Noah.

Camille wiped her hands on her napkin. "I told them we'd dance after dinner, but they have no patience."

Maddie couldn't dance with Lucas. She was already getting in too deep with him, and her heart could only take so much. It was still pounding in her chest from the misunderstanding.

Camille talked about Noah and the ranch over dinner, but Maddie couldn't bring herself to speak much. She had no idea how to handle her feelings for Lucas, and navigating their growing relationship was getting harder by the day.

When the waitress had taken their empty plates, Camille waved Noah and Lucas over to their table. "You're free to join us now. Girl time is over."

"Did you talk about us?" Lucas asked as he slid in beside Maddie.

"Yes, but mostly how to get the smell out of your boots," Camille said.

Lucas smiled. "You like us."

Camille sighed as Noah extended his hand to her. "See you on the dance floor."

Lucas turned to Maddie and dramatically offered her his hand. "May I have this dance?"

Maddie scanned the room for a way out but found none. "I don't know how to dance."

"Just let me lead."

Asher's smooth voice filled the room with the beginnings of a slow song, and Maddie was at war with herself. She could manage her way through a slow dance, but her heart might not make it out unscathed.

Before she knew what she was doing, her hand was wrapped in his and he was leading her to the crowd of people moving to the music. His hand rested against the small of her back, and the thin cotton of her dress did nothing to protect her skin from the searing heat.

"I knew you could dance," he said.

Maddie shook her head. "I've never danced before."

Lucas's mouth stretched to one side in that grin she adored. Would she ever get over him? She had to. Feeling this much this soon—it was the worst thing that could have happened to her after taking the job at Blackwater Ranch.

"You're a natural. Just move with the music," Lucas instructed.

Being this close to Lucas made her want to melt into him. The inches between them begged to be erased.

Feeling like this—feeling anything for Lucas— was a bad idea. She needed to keep her job, and getting close to him would make her comfortable. If she trusted him, she'd slip up and tell him about her parents, and the Hardings would have her out of that new cabin in no time.

Maddie stepped back, unsure what her body was doing.

"Maddie?"

"I need a minute," she said before pushing her way through the crowd of people toward the restrooms.

Once inside the private room, she stared at herself in the mirror.

"I can't do this," she whispered to herself. Covering her face with her hands, she took deep breaths and prayed.

"Lord, why is it so hard for me to let someone in? I want to be happy, but I'm terrified." Other people flirted and dated and seemed happy in relationships. She'd never experienced that kind of freedom before. "I just want to be myself. Not what my parents made me think I am."

Maddie raised her head and groaned at the red eyes staring back at her. Great, Lucas would know she was upset.

She closed her eyes and blocked out everything. "I've survived everything else. I can get through this. God is with me."

A few minutes later, she stepped out of the women's bathroom and almost walked right into Lucas.

"I'm so sorry. I didn't know you were standing there."

Lucas grinned, but the expression was strained. "Everything okay? You ran off pretty quickly."

"I'm fine." Surprisingly, her voice was steady, and she felt calm. "I think I need to get home though. I'm tired after moving my stuff all day."

"I'll take you home." Lucas extended his arm to her, and she took it, promising herself that it was harmless to accept a ride since they were headed to the same place.

They caught Camille and Noah's attention on the dance floor and let them know they were leaving. Maybe the loud music was adding to her anxiety because she started to feel better as they left the dance floor.

They were almost to the exit when a petite brunette grabbed Lucas's other arm.

"Lucas! Dance with me!"

Maddie was instantly uncomfortable. She was keeping Lucas from having fun tonight, and the words tumbled out of her mouth quickly. "You can stay. I'll just hang out in Camille's car until she's ready to leave."

"Sorry, Ansley," Lucas said without hesitation. "I'm taking Maddie home, but it's good to see you."

"Oh." Ansley's smile faded. "Maybe next time."

Lucas tipped his imaginary hat. "See you later."

Maddie followed Lucas to his truck and slid into the dark cab. He didn't strike up conversation, and she was certain the quiet drive back was because he regretted leaving Ansley. She was a pretty woman and obviously interested in him. Maddie had just dampened his fun. She seemed to do little else these days. He'd spent his free time fixing up a place for her to stay, and then he'd helped her move in. All he did with her was work, and Lucas was a fun-loving creature by nature.

They were almost back to the ranch when Lucas finally spoke up. "Did you have fun tonight?"

"Of course. Camille is sweet, and I like her. I'm sorry I wasn't a better dancer."

Lucas reached for her hand. "I loved dancing

with you. I'm always happy when I'm with you. Somehow, you even have a way of making work enjoyable."

Maddie couldn't speak. Lucas soothed her wounds with his words, and she had no idea how to respond to his kindness.

He parked the truck in front of her cabin and shut off the diesel engine. Her hand rested comfortably in his, and he turned it over. He touched the sensitive skin of her open palm and traced circles there before lining every finger.

The slight tickle sent shocks up her arm, and she wanted more. Adrenaline pulsed through her veins as he drew on her skin.

"Are you okay?" he asked softly.

Maddie nodded and then realized he couldn't see her in the darkness. The only light around was from the Christmas lights lining his cabin fifty yards away.

"Yeah. I'm fine." She dropped her gaze to their hands. "I'm really just figuring out how to fit in around here."

"You're doing fine. I know you're tired, but would you like to meet me in the morning for a surprise?"

"Before church?" Maddie asked.

"Yeah, at dawn. We'll be back with plenty of time to get ready for church."

"Okay then. You're not going to tell me what we're doing?"

"Nope. You'll have to meet me to find out."

"Where and when?"

Lucas linked his fingers between hers and gripped her hand. "I'll pick you up at sunrise."

Oh, a romantic setting. That probably wasn't a good idea when Lucas was involved.

"I'll be here," she confirmed.

"Thank you. I know you'd rather sleep in on your off day."

That wasn't the case. She'd rather wake up before the cows with Lucas than sleep in.

She opened the door and slid from the truck, whispering, "See you in the morning."

Despite her exhaustion, she might not get any sleep tonight anticipating tomorrow.

CHAPTER 15
LUCAS

Lucas was up well before the sun. His morning date with Maddie required extensive preparation. Just after sunrise, he parked in front of Maddie's cabin and sprinted to her door.

She answered promptly after his first rapping knock and looked around him. "How did you get here?"

"I drove," Lucas said uncertainly. "I feel like this is a trick question."

"I just heard you pull up, but you could've walked over. Did you go somewhere?"

He held up the white bag between them. "I brought you something."

She grabbed the bag excitedly. "You brought me a doughnut! You went to Sticky Sweet's this morning?"

Lucas shrugged, secretly pleased with her reaction. "I've been up for a while."

Her T-shirt read *Hold your horses*, but she reached for a jean jacket hanging by the door and hung it over her arm. "Let's do this, cowboy."

She'd barely settled into her seat in the truck before she ripped open the bag revealing the glazed sweets.

"You got two. You want yours now?" she asked.

"They're both for you."

Maddie shook her head. "I can't eat two."

"Why not?"

Maddie narrowed her eyes at him.

Lucas made a *tsk* sound behind his teeth. "I know you're not about to say something about your weight. We don't need that kind of negativity on this date. Eat the doughnuts."

She shoved the first bite into her mouth and closed her eyes. "They're so good," she mumbled.

She was wiping her sticky fingers on the napkins as he parked at the stables.

"You gave me a ride to work. How sweet," she said with faux pleasantness.

"You think you're so funny. We're not working. We're riding. I've already groomed and prepped the horses."

Maddie paused. "You really have been up a while."

Lucas checked his watch. "We have a few hours to wander before we have to eat and get ready for church, and this is the best time of day for riding." The weather was moderate in the mornings in late September, but midday could be a little warm on sunny days.

She sought out Dolly, and Lucas caught her sneaking the animal a treat. She nuzzled Dolly's cheek and whispered good morning.

There were lots of horse lovers in Blackwater. Horses were a normal part of life here. Rodeos and trail rides were a dime a dozen. Somehow, Maddie stood out from other people. Lucas hadn't met a woman who shared his all-out passion for the gentle giants until Maddie.

He hadn't made any great effort to date yet. He'd always assumed there would be time for that later. There was a season for everything, and Lucas still hadn't found that season of life where he found someone to commit to.

He watched Maddie as she interacted with Dolly and realized that she had changed his focus. He'd been praying about the shift he felt in his life, and the Lord didn't seem to be urging him to steer clear of her. On the contrary, his time with Maddie felt significant and important as if God were telling him to pay attention.

After working two jobs, there wasn't much left of him, but he found himself wanting to spend every second of that time with her. Things were different when he and Maddie occupied the same spaces every day. He didn't have to divide his time when she was always beside him. In fact, he sought her out more times than not. He could have the best of both worlds—the jobs and woman he loved.

Loved? The thought was sudden but not unwelcome. The leather of her saddle creaked, and he watched her riding Dolly from the stables, the golden sunrise creating a glow around her that amplified his revelation.

He loved Maddie Faulkner, and he wondered how long he'd have to wait until she was ready to know.

M addie laughed high and loud in the open morning air. "How long did you stay in there?"

Lucas had filled their morning ride with stories from his childhood on the ranch. When they'd passed the barn in the western pasture, he told her about the time Asher had pushed him over the high wall of the corn catch and left him.

"He let it slip to Micah where I was. I was only there for maybe half an hour."

"What did you do?" she asked, enthralled by his childhood mishaps.

"I remember singing a few George Strait tunes to myself and trying to stack the cobs up against the exit wall to climb out. That was never going to work. I was maybe nine years old."

They entered the stables and Lucas slid off Weston. "I think we missed breakfast, but Mama might have some leftovers we can grab."

"I think the doughnuts were enough for me, but I'll go with you. Something might catch my eye." Maddie stepped into Dolly's stall with the horse and let out a high-pitched squeal a moment later.

Lucas jerked at the sound, but a startled Weston stepped toward him, knocking Lucas off balance and onto his back. He hit the stall floor with a thud that knocked the air from his lungs, and the horse promptly stepped on his ankle.

His cry of pain was a muffled "argh" followed by a few choice words for the horse.

Maddie frantically ran around the stall and crouched beside him. "Are you okay?" Her eyes were wide, and she shifted her attention back and forth along his body.

"I'm fine. Are you okay? I heard you scream."

"Dolly just spooked me. You're hurt. I'll call Noah."

Lucas waved her off. "No. None of that. Crazy horse just stepped on my ankle." He pushed to his feet with Maddie's assistance and tested his weight on the injured ankle. "He really just grazed it. My boots might have helped. I think there might be blood but no broken bones."

Maddie's breathing was still elevated, and he rested a hand on her shoulder. "Hey, relax. I'm okay."

Her cheeks had lost their color, and she wore a stern expression. "Don't scare me like that."

"Honey, that was nothing. We get hurt all the time around here."

"That doesn't mean I shouldn't care!"

He pulled her into a hug and rocked her body back and forth. "I'm glad you care."

Silence followed their declarations, and the tension in her body gradually melted away.

She stepped back and brushed a hand over her braid. "I may have overreacted." Her lips quirked up on one side, and the look she gave him was nothing short of flirting.

Lucas fought to contain his grin. "Just a little." He squeezed his thumb and index finger together, indicating the lack of space between them.

She pushed his chest playfully and turned her back on him. "Stop it."

Lucas scrambled to catch up with her. "Hey, remember that time you thought I was dying?"

"Ugh," she grunted. "You're impossible."

"Too soon?"

"Too soon," she confirmed.

Too soon seemed to be the broken record between them. Was it too soon for jokes or too soon to tell her how he felt about her?

CHAPTER 16
MADDIE

Maddie woke the next morning with a start and a pounding in her chest. She'd gone to the stables after supper last night to have some time to herself and remembered she'd left her journal.

Throwing on jeans and a sweater, she chastised herself on the way out the door. How could she have been so careless? That book held her innermost thoughts about *everything* that mattered to her.

Talking to the horses always calmed her, but she'd taken her journal and prayed too. Unfortunately, she'd forgotten the book after saying her good nights to the few horses that were stabled for the night.

It wasn't breakfast time yet, and she only passed one truck at the main house. It was barely daylight, but her heart sank when she spotted Lucas's truck at the stables.

What was he doing here this early? Whatever he was doing could wait until her workday started. How often did he check on the horses early in the morning before she woke? Didn't he trust her?

The thud of her truck door slamming pierced the quiet morning, and her long, tangled hair blew in the early-morning breeze as she sprinted for the door. *Please, Lord, let the journal be where I left it.*

That book was one of many she'd written over the years, but it was completely private. The contents were for her and God alone, and the thought of Lucas reading her private prayers had her stomach turning.

He stepped out of the office when she ran in. "Good morning. You're early."

Panting, she ran her hand through her messy hair as she scanned the area. It wasn't on the bench where she'd left it. Her gaze darted around the stables in search of the book. "Yeah. I left something here, and I came to get it."

"Oh, this?" Lucas turned back to the desk in his office and picked up her journal. "I found it on the bench."

"Did you... did you read it?" she asked as she took it from him.

Lucas laughed. "You think highly of me. I've been here for ten minutes. I'm not a slow reader, but I'm not finishing a book in less than a week."

Heat rose in Maddie's cheeks. "Be serious, Lucas. Did you read any of it?"

Lucas stilled, and she knew her tone had held accusation.

"No, I really didn't." He crossed his arms over his chest and settled his stance. "It isn't mine."

Maddie bit at her fingernail. Staring down at the journal, she knew Lucas would be acting much differently if he'd read it. He'd know all about her parents and the dark secrets she held.

Lucas stepped toward her and reached out a hand to touch her shoulder before changing his mind and letting it fall. "Are you okay?"

She knew he hadn't read it. Not only because he wasn't accusing her of being an accessory to a crime against his family, but because she knew in her heart that Lucas respected boundaries. He'd been patient and allowed her to guard her heart since she came here. Why would she question him?

"I'm sorry. I know you didn't read it. It's just..."

"Private?" Lucas asked. "I get it. You're allowed to have thoughts and feelings that you don't share with me. I won't ever require you to give more than you're willing. I know you're not an open book, but I'm not going to pry into your life to learn about you. I'm a patient man, and you can tell me things in your own time or not at all."

Maddie swallowed hard. An acidic tingle burned her throat and behind her eyes.

She trusted him. That rare and precious understanding now stood between them, and it changed everything.

Why did it make her want to open her heart to him?

She hadn't been able to trust her parents to stick around for her, but she trusted this man not to steal her most private thoughts when she'd left them accessible to him.

Lucas raised his hand again, and this time, he did brush it over her shoulder. "Whatever you write in there, you can share it with me if you want. I don't want you to think I'm not going to be here for you. No matter what it is, I'll be by your side."

Did he know what he was saying? People always left. The people God had tied her to on this earth by blood hadn't stayed.

Yet, Lucas was saying he wouldn't be moved, and it was terrifying.

Unsure of what to say or do, she stepped away from him. His hand fell from her shoulder and back to his side. His smile fell just as abruptly.

"I need to get ready for breakfast. I'll see you then." Maddie backed out of the office and quickened her pace to the exit.

When she was safe inside her truck, she sucked in breaths and willed the tears to stay. There was something about being accepted for who she was by someone who had no obligation to care about her that had the walls around her heart crumbling.

Her mom and dad had liked stealing more than they'd loved their daughter, but a sweet cowboy with a kind heart was putting it all on the line for her.

It didn't seem real, but oh did she want it to be. Her tired and lonely heart wanted to be cherished, and Lucas was beginning to look a lot like home.

CHAPTER 17

LUCAS

Lucas was up and ready before the sun, but the call of the morning wasn't as strong as usual. Maddie had been upset yesterday morning, and she'd avoided him for the rest of the day. Unsure what else to say to assure her that he hadn't read the diary, he hadn't said anything.

Of course Maddie kept a diary. Everyone needed to get things off their chests, and when things were hard to say, they were often easier to write. As much as he wished she'd share her feelings with him, he couldn't read her secrets when he hadn't been invited.

He'd spent his life training horses and waiting patiently for their acceptance. He could definitely wait and show Maddie he was on her side.

Waiting wasn't so bad. He didn't have any

reason to rush. Things didn't change much on the ranch, but he'd developed a new longing since Maddie showed up in his life.

Breakfast was about to start, and Maddie wasn't anywhere to be found. Surely, she wasn't still upset with him. He hadn't actually read the diary, but maybe he'd misunderstood the conversation. Was she mad because he'd moved it?

When they couldn't wait any longer for breakfast, he called her. As the rings echoed in his ear, he was already walking toward the door. Panic stirred his thoughts. What if she left? Had she really not intended to stay from the start?

He could see the stables, and her truck wasn't there. With only one place left to check, he jumped in the truck and headed for her cabin. If she wasn't there, then he had reason to worry.

Her truck was parked out front, and he breathed a sigh of relief. She wasn't required to show up for breakfast, and maybe she hadn't wanted to see him this morning. Assuming he owed her an apology, Lucas knocked on the door.

Maddie's muffled voice rose from the other side of the door. "It's open."

Lucas stepped into the dark cabin, but he didn't see much. "Maddie?"

Quiet sniffles came from inside the room, and Maddie said, "Over here."

He turned on the lights and stepped around the couch. Maddie was lying on her back with her hands over her face.

"Maddie? What's wrong?" He tended to worry over Maddie an excessive amount, but today his worries were founded in reality. He sat on the floor beside the couch and brushed her hair from her face. "Maddie, please talk to me."

"I'm sorry." Her words were muffled by her hands. "It's my back. I can't get up, and my phone is over there." She pointed toward the kitchen table where her phone sat. She covered her face again and sobbed loudly. "I fell asleep here last night, and I must have slept wrong because I can't get up."

"Don't try to move. Just tell me what to do."

Maddie cried, and Lucas waited a moment before laying his hand on her arm. "Maddie. Let me help you. What do you need?"

She finally wiped her eyes with her hands and the backs of her arms. "Can you get your parents on the phone? I need to tell them I can't make it to the stables today."

"Sure." Lucas dialed Asher's number, knowing his parents wouldn't have a phone on them during breakfast.

Asher answered on the second ring. "Hey. You find her?"

"Yeah. She's having some back trouble, and she

wants to talk to Mom. Can you hand her the phone?"

"Sure."

When he heard his mom answer, Lucas passed the phone to Maddie.

"Mama Harding? I'm so sorry, but I woke up this morning with back trouble. I haven't been able to get up, and..." Maddie's tears started again, and she gritted her teeth trying to hold them in. "I don't think I can make it to the stables today."

Maddie nodded as his mother spoke and ended the call with a promise to update her later. She handed the phone back to Lucas and wiped her face on the blanket wrapped around her. "I'm so sorry. This is embarrassing."

"It's nothing to be embarrassed about. We're all getting older. Some of us just age faster than others."

Maddie chuckled and brushed her hair from her face. "Funny."

"Seriously, it happens to all of us. Noah has a leg that gives him trouble, Micah has trouble with a knee he pretty much shattered when he was twenty, and Aaron has to take time off when Levi needs him." Lucas shrugged. "We all need sick days."

"Thanks," she whispered.

"Now, what do you need?"

"I don't really know. I tried to get up earlier, and it didn't go so well." She averted her gaze and rubbed the fringes of the quilt between her fingers. "I was in a wreck when I was young, and I had a back injury. It wasn't terrible, but now I sometimes get muscle spasms. They last for about a day, but during that time, I'm worthless."

It was the most she'd ever told him about her past, and he soaked up every word. "So, are we trying to get you to a doctor today, or are we just maintaining until the pain passes?"

"Oh, you're not doing anything. I'll be fine here. I just need to not do anything."

"Except eat and go to the bathroom. I don't think you can do those things on your own, so I'll be staying."

"No, Lucas. Someone has to take care of the horses today."

"No problem. Asher knows the drill. I just need to call him."

Maddie's face was pink and splotchy from her tears, and she blew out a breath that puffed her cheeks. "I don't want you to have to do that."

"It's really no problem. Asher knows what he's doing. I'll be right back."

Lucas stepped outside to call his brother. The rising sun blanketed the hillside in a red glow that meant they could expect a storm later. The old adage, "Red sky in the morning, sailors take warning. Red sky at night, sailor's delight," held enough truth that Lucas believed it.

His brother was quick to answer again, and Lucas gave him instructions for the day. Asher knew plenty about the horses, but he needed new instructions for Dolly.

When he stepped back inside, Maddie had discarded the blanket and was pulling on the back of the couch.

"What are you doing?" Lucas asked.

Maddie pursed her lips and averted her eyes. "I need to use the bathroom."

"I'll help you."

"No!" Maddie yelped. "I just need to figure out how to get up. I can do it."

"Don't worry. I'll leave you to the mechanics on your own, but I can at least help you get there."

Maddie looked like she wanted to cry again. "I don't want to do this."

He knelt down beside her and squirmed his arms beneath her shoulders and knees. "Your job is to tell me if something I do hurts. Okay?"

She didn't look at him as she nodded.

Lifting her slowly to minimize jarring, Lucas only had to stop to readjust his grip once when she cried out in pain. When he'd made it to standing, she was much easier to carry without jostling if he held her tight against his chest. What he wouldn't give to be able to touch her and hold her like this without a debilitating injury.

Her body was warm and soft against his hard

chest. It felt like carrying an armload of linens straight from the dryer. When she tucked her head into the crook of his neck, he breathed in her smell of cedarwood. She never smelled like a flower or something girly, but an overly feminine scent wouldn't reflect the true Maddie. She was just as likely to get her hands dirty on the ranch as she was to braid her long blonde hair in the morning, and Lucas wouldn't change that about her.

In fact, he wouldn't change anything about her, but he'd keep hoping she'd open up to him eventually. One day, he'd like to be able to tell her how he felt without sending her running for the hills.

He slowly set her on her feet in the bathroom doorway, but even his easy movements didn't prevent her sudden yelps of pain. When she was out of his arms, he held her for a moment to make sure she was steady. Her teeth were gritted, and a light sheen of sweat coated her forehead.

Her words shook as she said, "I've got it from here."

Lucas stepped back, letting his hand fall from her arm, and closed the door. He hated seeing her in pain. It was worse than living with the pain himself.

His thoughts had traveled to a place he didn't recognize. He hadn't necessarily lived a selfish life, but he'd never had someone who meant as much to him as Maddie. Rubbing a hand over his jaw, he propped his back against the wall and waited for her to finish.

When she opened the door, her gaze was downcast. Her braid had been fixed, but her eyes were tired and puffy.

From where he stood, Maddie seemed to have life figured out. She was determined and focused to a fault, and being tied down and helpless was probably the worst scenario for her.

Cradling her lower back in one hand and the side of her face in another, she asked, "Do we have to do the carrying?"

"No, we don't have to." It had seemed like the easiest and least painful solution to him, but if she was uncomfortable being close to him, he wouldn't subject her to it again.

She reached out a hand for the support of his arm, and he moved slowly beside her as she stepped out of the bathroom. After three tentative steps, she jerked and let out a pain-filled yell.

Lucas bit his lip in frustration. Knowing she was in pain and he couldn't help was torture.

Maddie covered her mouth and breathed hard through her nose. "I don't think I can do this."

"Do you want me to carry you?" When she didn't respond right away, he closed his eyes and said a silent prayer that she would trust him with this one thing. Seeing her in pain was making his stomach turn.

Finally, she answered. "Okay."

Picking her up from standing was much harder. He took his time, testing the static strength of every muscle in his body, but she still cried out twice before he could get her to the couch on her back.

"Are you sure I can't take you to a doctor?" Lucas asked.

"I'm really going to be okay." She wiped her eyes. "It hasn't ever lasted more than a day."

"What do you do while you wait?"

Maddie tugged at her braid. "Heat and cold. Sometimes I take an anti-inflammatory, but I don't like taking medicine unless I have to."

Her treatment method seemed extremely conservative, but what did he know about muscle spasms? "Okay. Do you have heat and ice packs?"

She directed him to the freezer and a cabinet in the bathroom. He returned with the packs and she chose the heat first. Slipping the pad beneath her back, she whispered, "Thank you."

"You're welcome."

"I don't have a TV," she reminded him.

Lucas grinned. "I'm aware. I'm your entertainment for the day."

Maddie rolled her eyes, but she seemed to be relaxing. "I'm sorry I've been so snappy. I just hate this whole situation."

Lucas leaned forward in his seat, propping his

elbows on his knees. "I know. This won't keep you down forever."

Maddie squeezed her eyes closed and pinched the bridge of her nose. On the verge of crying again, she nodded and laid her hand over her eyes.

Lucas stood. "I'm going to give you a minute to relax while I make breakfast."

Maddie's muffled "Thank you" was enough to send him to the kitchen. He opened the fridge and cabinets and found little he could throw together to make a decent breakfast. She ate most meals at the main house, so there wasn't much need to keep food around.

"I'll be right back," he shouted as he grabbed his jacket. "Don't go anywhere."

He heard her low chuckle as he closed the door behind him and sprinted to his house. He grabbed some bacon, eggs, and a loaf of bread and headed back to her place to cook. When breakfast was ready, he plated the meal and went to check on her. She seemed considerably calmer when he returned. She removed the heat pad, and he helped her sit up. She sucked in a few breaths through her teeth, but she didn't yell this time.

"Are you eating too?" she panted once she was upright.

"I'll eat a bite in a minute." In truth, he was too shaken up by Maddie's ailment to stomach anything.

"This looks delicious. Does your mama know you can cook?"

Lucas winked. "She taught me all I know. Mamas get sick too, and she always said we should know how to do each other's jobs."

"Like how Asher can take care of the horses today?"

"Exactly. We mostly switch things up on a regular basis around here, but we all have our strengths."

"Like what?"

"Noah is a natural at running machinery. Micah is the mechanic. I have a way with the horses." Lucas ticked off each example on his fingers. "Things like that."

Maddie shoved a piece of bacon into her mouth like she hadn't eaten in days, and he left her to her meal while he googled treatments for muscle spasms on his phone.

The first recommendation from Doctor Google was a gentle massage of the spasming area. Unable to resist, Lucas questioned, "So, were you going to tell me that massages help relieve muscle spasms?"

Maddie's eyes grew round. "No, I wasn't."

"I think we should give that a try after breakfast."

"No!" she shouted. "I mean, I just think I'll be okay."

Lucas laughed. "Relax. I'm not in the business of

taking advantage of injured women. But I would be willing to help out any way I can."

Maddie saw through his attempt at humor and pursed her lips to hide her smile. "You're the worst."

"I think you're confused. I'm the best."

She playfully threw the last piece of bacon at him. When he caught it and shoved it in his mouth, she looked like she might laugh or cry at any moment.

"Listen," Lucas said, taking her plate. "I think you should take a nap if you can. The rest might do you some good."

Maddie nodded. "I think I will. You don't have to stay."

"I think I'll grab a measuring tape out of my truck and measure for the shelves in the kitchen cabinets. Then I'll go get the wood out of the north barn."

"Okay. Can you help me lie back down?"

Lucas cradled the weight of her upper body as he eased her to a lying position.

"Lucas," she said, touching his arm while he knelt beside her.

"Yeah." Whatever she needed, he was prepared to fetch it for her.

"I'm sorry again... and for yesterday. You didn't do anything wrong. I was just scared."

He touched the hair at her temple before letting

his fingers trail along her jaw to her chin. "I know. Just rest. I'll take care of everything."

For the time being, he could build shelves for her —anything to show her he would be sticking around.

CHAPTER 18
LUCAS

A little over an hour later, Maddie was stirring on the couch. She made little stretches and noises as she woke up, and Lucas kept his place in the tattered old recliner, far too interested in the small movements she made while coming out of sleep.

She sniffed and patted her braid. "You're still here."

"I went out to get the supplies, but I didn't want to wake you when I started banging around in the kitchen."

She tried to sit up but sucked in a breath through her teeth at the movement. "It's not as bad as earlier, but I'm still stuck here."

"Maybe you should take another nap. I was getting used to the lulling rhythm of your snores."

Her mouth gaped. "You were not. I don't snore."

Lucas gave her a skeptical look. "Says you." He slapped his knees and stood. "What do you need before I get to work?"

Maddie's gaze darted toward the bathroom. "Would you mind helping me up again?"

Lucas grinned. "You need only ask, and I'll gladly sweep you off your feet, pretty lady."

She was laughing when he slipped his hands beneath her and began lifting. This time, she didn't cry out in pain, and he called it a win.

When she was finished, he cradled her in his arms again and carried her to the couch. He helped her get settled and then asked, "Now what?"

Maddie raised her hands, palms up. "I don't know. I never sit around all day, so I don't even have books to read."

He made a quick assessment of the small space before picking up one end of the couch.

"What are you doing?" she asked, grabbing the parts of the furniture she could reach.

"I'm going to install shelving in the kitchen cabinets, and you're coming with me."

He picked up the other end and swung the couch around at the edge of the small kitchen. "There. Now we can keep each other company, and you can tell me how you want things done around here."

"Somehow, I feel like I'm in a position of power right now," Maddie said. "Lucas Harding is carrying me around, entertaining me with his woodworking skills, and taking orders."

Lucas began fitting the boards into the cabinets. "You hit the jackpot today. Should I take my shirt off and give you a real show?"

She leveled him with a menacing stare. "Keep your clothes on, Casanova."

Lucas looked over his shoulder to find a beautiful blush covering her neck and cheeks. "Suit yourself."

Maddie stayed relatively still and horizontal for the rest of the morning while he installed the shelves. It was nearly noon when he finished and his mother called to check on Maddie.

He stepped outside to give her some privacy and call his brother. Asher had texted for an update on Maddie's injury, but it was faster to call.

"Hey, are we gonna have to trade her in for a newer model?" Asher asked.

"Not yet. She's hanging' in there. I think we'll keep her."

"Good. Is she itching to get out of there?"

"Don't you know it. Keeping her happy on the couch is like roping a calf."

Asher laughed. "You need me to bring lunch?"

Lucas stood and stepped back inside. "I don't know. Let me ask her."

She was off the phone and looked up when he entered.

"You want Asher to bring us lunch?"

Her gaze darted around the kitchen. "I actually had my heart set on a peanut butter and jelly sandwich."

Lucas brought the phone back to his ear. "That's a negative, bro. The lady wants fine dining."

"Suit yourself. I'll check back in at suppertime."

Lucas stuck the phone back in his pocket and rubbed his hands together. "So, peanut butter and jelly?"

"Yes, please."

Lucas made the sandwiches in an elated haze. Not many adults would choose a peanut butter and jelly sandwich for a meal, but Maddie knew it was his favorite. Her consideration had his body humming with affection for her. He wasn't going to find another woman like Maddie, no matter how many years he spent on this earth. God had made Maddie for Lucas, and he just needed to tell her and hope he didn't scare her away.

When he turned around with the plated sandwiches, a lump rose into his throat, constricting the words he wanted to say. Why was he terrified to tell her how he felt? Probably because he'd moved right from casual interest to love without skipping a beat. Something about her timid reserve had him holding back.

"Looks delicious," Maddie said.

Lucas helped her to a sitting position, hyper

aware of her breath on his neck. His breath was shaky as he sat beside her, unnaturally silent.

"You okay?" she asked.

Sure, if you discounted the heart palpitations, sweating, and shortness of breath. "Of course."

"You look pale."

Lucas shook his head. "I'm fine."

"Don't go dying on me. I'm helpless without you."

Maddie's smile bloomed, and Lucas began to relax. This was Maddie. He didn't need to be anything but himself around her. No rush to tell her of his undying love or anything else that kept him up at night.

He said a blessing over the food and took the first bite before moaning in delight. "This is delicious."

"Are you bragging on your own sandwich making skills? A five-year-old could do the same."

"Just let me enjoy this moment," Lucas murmured around the sticky peanut butter in his mouth. "I deserve a trophy for this creation."

Maddie laughed, and the musical tone filled the small cabin. Lucas would lay everything on the line for a life like this with her.

After lunch, Lucas lowered Maddie back onto the couch before cleaning up. He asked her simple questions about her life. Where did she go to college? Where did she barrel race? What was her favorite movie? Was she a morning or a night person?

He took anything she was willing to give him and let it fill him up. While they talked, he used the extra materials he'd brought to add shelving to the small linen closet in her bathroom.

Later in the day, Asher called as promised, and Maddie and Lucas both requested dinner. Half an hour later, a knock at the door announced their delivery.

When Lucas answered the door, he wasn't surprised to see his cousin, Hunter, carrying two large bags of food. The sky was a menacing charcoal gray behind him, promising the storm Lucas had predicted this morning. The air even smelled sweet and charged, ready to unload any minute.

"Thanks for this. Is that meatloaf I smell?"

Hunter nodded as thunder rumbled in the distance. "It was pretty good too. Anita sent extra helpings."

Lucas took the bags and pointed toward the shadowed horizon with his chin. "You better get going."

Hunter tipped his hat and stepped back to his truck before Lucas closed the door with his foot. He set the bags on the table before carefully carrying Maddie to the kitchen. She didn't make a peep, but he thought she held tighter to his shoulders this time.

Maddie was quieter as they ate, and he wanted to dismiss the nervous pricking in his stomach. Was she getting tired of having him around? It had only been a day.

After the meal, she called Mama Harding to thank her for the food while he cleaned up.

Once the dishes were clean, he turned to her, propping on the counter behind him with a nonchalance he didn't feel. "So, what would you like to do now?" The rain on the old roof of the cabin pelted relentlessly. It sounded like a river rushing over the ancient structure.

"I'd like to watch the rain, if you don't mind."

Lucas nodded and bent to lift her into his arms. She stopped him short with a hand extended toward him.

"I think I can move on my own. I'd like to try, but I might need a little help."

Concealing the rejection that struck him harder than a branding iron, Lucas extended his arm for her to brace on as she lifted herself from the chair.

She stood on her own and grinned, but the expression was pained. "I think it's starting to subside. I've rested more today than I usually do when this happens."

Slowly, Lucas helped her to the porch and lowered her into a rocking chair with his arm supporting her back. Lightning lit the dark sky just before thunder boomed through the air, echoing off the distant hills.

"I love watching the rain," Maddie said as she rocked.

Lucas took the chair beside her but couldn't force his stare from her. "Why?"

She sighed. "I lived with Aunt Brenda in Montgomery, Alabama once. I was about twelve, and I wasn't talking a lot." Maddie hung her head and twirled the end of her braid between her fingers. "It rained constantly the first season we lived there, and my aunt used to ask me to sit in the front porch swing with her when it rained. She said it would drown the doubts." Maddie looked up at him. "You can't hear your thoughts over the pounding rain."

Lucas leaned closer to her over the arm of the rocking chair. "What thoughts are you trying not to hear?"

Maddie looked toward the main house. "I was just thinking about Hunter."

"What?" Lucas asked. He hadn't expected her to be thinking of his cousin.

"It's just that he has that scar, and I feel... bad. I sit around in a pity party a lot feeling all woe is me, but some people have bigger problems." She tucked her chin and shook her head. "It's stupid."

No, it wasn't stupid at all. Lucas wanted to know what had hurt her, physical scars or not, but he also knew he would never get there if he didn't give what he wanted to get in return.

Lucas steeled his resolve and confessed, "It was my fault."

Maddie's braid fell from her shoulder at the jerk of her head. "What?"

"Hunter's injury." Lucas scrubbed a hand over his face. This wasn't something he liked talking about, but he needed to give more of himself to her. It felt right, but it also felt like a squirrel was trapped in his stomach.

The rain was falling in thick sheets now, and loud enough that he would have to raise his voice to be heard over the roaring. There would be no whispered confessions here, and certainly no hiding from his thoughts.

"We were young, and a lot was going on back then that I didn't understand. Hunter's dad used to live here too, but one day his dad disappeared out of the blue. He'd stolen more than this ranch could afford to lose and left his son behind."

Maddie stiffened and gripped the chair. "When did this happen?"

"I was ten and Hunter was sixteen. So, you probably hadn't been gone a few years."

Maddie didn't urge him on, but the tension in her shoulders told him to tread lightly.

"Our parents let us younger kids play on the ranch as long as we stayed close enough to come when they yelled for us. I was usually the one pushing the limits, and I went too far one day. A pack of wild dogs cornered me at the edge of the woods at sundown."

Lucas propped his elbows on his knees and hung his head. "I didn't have a weapon, and I was scared. Hunter heard me yelling and ran to help me, but the dogs didn't back down."

Maddie's hand rested on his back. Soothing warmth comforted him as he kept his gaze on the porch's floorboards.

"Hunter didn't have a weapon either. We usually always carry a gun around the ranch, but he was just tightening the hinge on a gate. He didn't think he'd need it." Lucas shook his head. "We don't make that mistake around here anymore."

"What did he do?" Maddie asked.

"He had two wrenches with him, and he banged them together and yelled at the dogs. They still didn't move. He had to get me out or distract the dogs, so he swung at one of them with the wrenches. They all attacked him."

Lucas could smell the blood. His nostrils flared as he fought to control the panic that accompanied the memory. The snarls and growls still woke him up at night.

It was better if he didn't sleep.

"He has other scars. Some are worse, but people

can't stare at those. Nothing has ever been easy for Hunter, and I made it worse."

The rain had slackened to a drizzle, but the runoff still trickled from the roof. She would think he was a screw-up now, and he prepared for the heartache that would follow her retreat.

Maddie's hand on his back began to move in calming circles. The innocence in the gesture had his heart begging to go to her. Just like that, he was a kid again. A kid who had made a huge, stupid mistake that almost cost his cousin his life.

"You were so young. People make mistakes, and you shouldn't carry the guilt your whole life."

Lucas lifted his head and turned to her. What was she saying? It was his fault.

"Have you talked to Hunter about it?" she asked.

"I apologized a lot... especially right after."

"What did he say?"

"He said not to worry about it."

"And you're still doing it."

"Well, yeah," Lucas said. He pointed toward the main house. "Did you see his face? Sorry doesn't erase that."

"No, but forgiveness does. I think what Hunter meant is that he has forgiven you."

Lucas shook his head. "He couldn't."

"Why not? Because you did something unworthy of forgiveness? We both know that's not true. God forgives us when we ask Him. Whether you've asked directly or not, He knows your heart. I think Hunter can see it too."

The hand caressing his back slid down his arm, and Lucas fought to breathe. How could she have known the exact words he'd needed to hear? His family had been telling him to forgive himself for years, so why did he finally want to listen when Maddie said it?

Because he wanted so badly to be worthy of her, and his past mistakes felt raw and dark when brought to light in front of her.

He looked at her as she squeezed his arm. A moment passed between them where he felt a shift.

"Lucas, I like you. I like you more than I should." She paused and huffed a deep breath. "But I'm scared."

It was finally happening. Now was the time to tell her about his feelings.

Maddie's hand moved across his arm, leaving coldness after her warmth that had his skin pebbling. When she reached his hand, she linked her fingers with his.

"There is something about this place. It's different. And it matters to me."

Her voice broke on the last word, and he wondered what she'd lost.

"The people here matter too," she continued. "I don't easily connect with people like I should. It's hard for me to trust or open up to anyone. It's not you. It's me." She chuckled, and the tension between them eased a little at her joke.

He couldn't tell her the extent of his feelings. She wasn't ready. But he could assure her of something.

"I like you too. Way more than you know. There isn't a reason to rush anything. I'll be here waiting when you're ready."

He would wait for her. She was worth every minute.

"I want to start... opening up to you. I want to have a chance here because I feel like life and all the good that I've found here will pass me by if I don't start looking at this as a blessing instead of a future with an ending."

Lucas squeezed her hand. "Just so you know, there isn't anything you're afraid of that could change how I feel about you."

He knew those words to be true in the deepest part of his heart. If there was something in her past she hid out of shame or guilt, his love could erase it. It was already gone, as far as he was concerned.

She scrunched her mouth to one side. "I don't really like the idea of dating my boss."

Lucas chuckled. "Don't worry. I'm not your boss. Technically, that's my parents' title."

Maddie laughed and pulled her hand back. Bracing her hands on the arms of the chair, she pushed up and slowly stood without the obvious pain from before.

She smiled at him, and he stood beside her. "Thank you for taking care of me today. I know I wouldn't feel as good as I already do if you hadn't waited on me hand and foot."

Lucas brushed the backs of his fingers across her cheek. "I would do anything for you."

He couldn't see her face in the darkness, but the silence around them was filled with ghosts of words he wanted to say. He wanted to kiss her, but he also wanted to see her reaction the first time. She'd just taken a big step with him, and he didn't want to push any boundaries. Instead, he threaded his fingers into her hair and kissed her forehead. Breathing in the fresh smell of the night washed by the rain, he lingered there, infusing his love into the touch.

He pulled away but leaned in close to her ear to whisper, "I know this hasn't been a good day for you, but I enjoyed every minute of it." After spending so much time with her, he didn't want to be without her. He knew he needed to walk the throwing distance to his cabin, but his feet wouldn't move.

"I enjoyed it too. If I hadn't been in pain, it would have been even better."

"Do you want me to stay?"

She was moving around on her own now, but that didn't mean she was able to do all the things she might need to do.

"I'm fine. Really. It's just an ache now." She rested her hands on her lower back and stretched slightly.

"I'm just right there. All you have to do is call, and I can be here in two minutes."

"Thank you. I'll see you in the morning."

"Good night," Lucas whispered.

"Good night."

He watched her walk inside before he meandered through the browning grass to his cabin. It was only a few steps, but it felt so far after a day spent growing closer to Maddie.

CHAPTER 19

MADDIE

The following Saturday was Levi's fourth birthday, and most talk of work was absent from the breakfast table. Instead of the usual balanced breakfast, Mama Harding made pancakes, French toast, and cinnamon rolls—all of Levi's favorites. She did sneak in some bacon for the grown men who had to spend the morning checking the herds and fences.

Maddie was thankful for Mama Harding's notice a week before the party. Everyone gave Levi a small gift after breakfast, and the boy's usual reserved demeanor was overruled by sugar and delight.

Watching him being chased by Lucas and Asher in the field beside the main house had a bubbly happiness rising from her toes to her ears. She remembered playing here with the Harding brothers when she was young, and she knew Levi would have a childhood worth remembering.

She still watched Hunter in silence, but instead of questions, her thoughts were filled with understanding. He'd thrown himself at the mercy of wild animals to protect his kin, and while she didn't know if she would ever have the courage to tell him how much she appreciated his sacrifice, he would always have her respect.

Lucas had told her a small bit of Hunter's story, but in a way, it had been Lucas's story. She'd learned more about him that night than in the weeks she'd been at Blackwater. That moment with Hunter and the dogs had shaped a young boy's character.

That day spent with Lucas had changed everything between them. She'd felt vulnerable and weak, but he'd leveled the playing field by sharing a painful part of his past. He'd exposed the emotional wounds he hid every day with his laughter and smiles, making her feel less alone.

Leaning against the wooden column on the front porch, Maddie watched Lucas playing tag with his nephew. He was attentive to the boy, and he could see his own playful nature in the younger Harding's eyes.

Not everyone had a way with kids, but Maddie loved them. Children were the hope for tomorrow, and she never wanted a child to feel unwanted or unloved. It was a risk to her heart to hope for kids of her own one day, but there were times when she watched Levi sneaking treats or out in the fields with the older Hardings and wished for a tiny human to share her love with.

Lucas caught Levi, wrapping him in a bear hug and twirling him around. Children had felt like a faraway dream for her—until now.

Lucas looked at her as if he'd sensed her watching him, and his smile was open and bright. Blackwater Ranch was a land covered in love and understanding, and she'd been too afraid to see it until now.

Mama Harding stepped out of the house, and her high whistle sliced through the air. "Load 'em up. Anyone going to town better get in the truck."

When the Harding boys had been young, Mama Harding started a tradition of taking each son to town on his birthday where he could pick out his own birthday gift and enjoy a mother-son day in Cody. Now, the tradition continued with Levi, and judging from the grin on Mama Harding's face, the day would be just as much for her as it was for the boys.

The rest of the family waved their good-byes as they trudged toward their trucks, ready for the day of work ahead. The sun was high in the sky, but the late-September wind was downright cold.

Maddie hugged her wool lined jean jacket tighter around her middle as Lucas stepped up to the porch where she waited. He touched her hand and hooked one of his fingers to hers.

"Thank you," he said.

"For what?" Maddie asked.

"For being so good to Levi. He's gonna love that rock tumbler you gave him."

Maddie shrugged. "What little boy doesn't like rocks?"

Lucas nodded and watched Aaron drive off. "Levi's mom left him when he was a baby. He sometimes has a hard time warming up to women. It's just Mom here, and Camille has been around for a little bit."

Maddie lifted the hand that linked them. "I know how he feels," she whispered.

"You never talk about your family."

Maddie squeezed his hand tighter. "My parents left me too. I don't want any kid to feel that."

Lucas released her hand and wrapped her in his arms. His warmth was as comforting as coming home on a cold day and snuggling in a pile of soft blankets on the bed.

"I'm sorry, Maddie. I don't know how anyone could ever leave you... or any kid."

"It's fine," she mumbled against his corduroy jacket. But it really wasn't. "It's just better if I don't get attached to anyone." Her chest was heavy and eyes full of sorrow as she looked up at him. "That way I'm not surprised when they leave."

Lucas shook his head and brushed his hand over her hair. "That's no way to live."

"It's the only way to live if you don't want a broken heart."

Lucas gently cupped her face in his hands, shielding her cheeks from the whipping wind. "Some people are meant to leave, but some are meant to stay."

Could he be one of those people she could be allowed to keep? She'd been praying, but she knew God's will for her was different from what she thought she wanted. Her childhood hadn't been an episode of *The Waltons* or *Little House on the Prairie*, but right now, she was happy in Lucas's arms. She got to watch Levi have the life she'd wanted for herself.

Levi's mom had left him, but the kid didn't seem to mind. He was surrounded by a family that loved him.

She hugged Lucas, resting her face against his chest and hoping he hadn't read her emotions. He dragged his fingers through her hair, careful not to disturb her braid. The motion soothed her into a calm she hadn't felt in years. How did he always know the kind of comfort she needed?

He had caring instincts. He'd grown up in a loving home and been shown love on a regular basis.

Lucas was going to be a wonderful husband and father one day.

The thought struck her in the chest like a pitchfork. Being a good parent wasn't something she expected of anyone. Her jaded past clouded her judgment and left her cynical. She knew the parenting instincts weren't ingrained in everyone. She'd lived through the proof.

Her phone buzzed in her jacket pocket, and she pulled away to check it.

"It's Aunt Brenda. I need to take this."

"Sure," Lucas said, kissing her forehead. "I'll see you at the stables later."

Waving to his retreating form, she answered the call. "Hello."

Aunt Brenda's throaty voice filled the line. "Maddie Bug!"

"How is everything?"

"I'm great. It's so good to hear your voice. I miss you like crazy."

"I miss you too."

After her parents were arrested, Aunt Brenda had fought for quick custody of Maddie and taken her in as her own. Maddie thanked the Lord every day for her only remaining family, and after traveling the country, moving every year or so for her aunt's job, they'd formed a bond that couldn't be broken.

"Good because I have a surprise," Brenda announced.

"What is it?" Her aunt's surprises, as well as everything else in her life, tended to be over the top. Moderation wasn't a word in Brenda's vocabulary.

"You get three guesses, and the last two don't count."

Maddie picked up the broom propped beside the door and began sweeping off the porch. "Um, your job is moving you again?"

"Not really. I'm taking a weekend off and coming to visit you."

"Really?" Maddie squealed. "That's great news!"

"Next weekend. Send me hotel recs, and none of that woodsy, roughing it stuff. You know what I like."

Aunt Brenda had worked her way to a successful career even while raising Maddie, and she had become accustomed to the finer things in life.

"I know. I'll ask around and text you later."

"I prefer a spa. Seriously, no dude ranches."

Maddie laughed, but the sound was drowned out by the rumble of Lucas's truck.

Unsure why he was back so soon, she cut the call short. "Got it. No semblance of real life."

"You know me so well," Brenda crooned.

"Sorry, but I have to go. My boss is pulling up. Talk to you soon. I love you."

"I love you too."

Maddie slipped the phone into her pocket just as Lucas bounded up the trio of stairs at the edge of the porch.

"You look like you're in a good mood," he said in greeting.

A few minutes ago, she'd been overwhelmed with concern for Levi and his motherless upbringing. Now, she was excited about the visit from her aunt next weekend.

"What are you doing back so soon?"

Lucas pointed toward his hat hanging on the nearby railing. "I left my hat. What's got you so happy?"

"My aunt Brenda is coming to visit."

"Great. Do I get to meet her?"

Maddie shrugged. "I don't know if that's a good idea."

Lucas scooted his foot around on the smooth boards of the porch. "So, would that be the equivalent of meeting your parents, since I can't do that?"

She hadn't told him the story of her parents yet, and the thought had a strip of panic rising up her spine. Maybe if she gave him a peek into her life, the fear of telling him the whole truth would subside.

"I guess you could say that. I moved in with her when I was ten and lived with her all through high school."

"Then I'll wear my Sunday best," Lucas declared.

"I didn't say you were meeting her." She tilted

her head at his sly maneuvering. "I think I said it wasn't a good idea."

Lucas's grin turned up on one side, and her gaze fell to his mouth. That grin was meant to melt knees. She found herself wondering what it would be like to kiss him.

"Are you afraid she'll fall for my charms?" he asked.

Maddie rolled her eyes and playfully shoved his chest. "I know the ladies can't resist you."

Lucas grabbed her hand and pulled her in close to whisper, "I'm only interested in one."

He pulled back slightly, and her heart pounded in her chest. She knew he was going to kiss her. He was close enough that she felt his warm breath on her face.

She was a string, pulled taut, waiting to snap.

His grin widened, and he stepped away from her, letting her hand fall from his.

He was driving her wild, and the rush she felt every time he almost kissed her left her wondering if she would burst into flames if his lips ever touched hers.

CHAPTER 20

LUCAS

Aunt Brenda was in town, and while Maddie had first told Lucas she wasn't ready for him to meet her aunt, she'd stopped by his cabin before leaving to meet Aunt Brenda and told him they were going to Barn Sour.

Snatching up the invitation, he'd promised to shower, shave, and be there within the hour.

He'd wanted to kiss her—for letting him in, for looking so gorgeous, and for trusting him with a part of her life she didn't let many people see.

On the drive to Barn Sour, his elation began to wane and was replaced by a nervous anxiety. The fear was new for him. He had a way with people and rarely felt overwhelmed in social situations, but meeting Maddie's aunt was a big deal, and he wanted to make the best impression. Maddie hadn't told him much about her aunt, and he was going in blind.

The parking lot was packed at Barn Sour, and he had to park in the back. By the time he made it inside, the live music was in full swing, and so were the couples dancing and flirting the night away.

He spotted Maddie's blonde hair from the doorway. She'd worn her hair down in long, soft waves that reminded him of a river of gold. He rarely saw her without her braid, especially now that the fall wind had given way to winter gales.

Maddie spotted him, but her reaction was minimal. Her smile may have been reserved, but her green eyes held a sparkle he wanted to bottle up and carry with him everywhere.

In response, the woman sitting across from her turned her entire body around to catch a glimpse of him before excitedly waving him over.

He stepped around tables and made his way to their booth against the wall opposite the stage. Lucas stopped at their table, unsure if he wanted to interrupt their reunion dinner completely. He could just meet her aunt and leave them to catch up.

"Have mercy. You must be Lucas," Aunt Brenda crooned. Her voice held a slight rasp, but it didn't diminish her friendliness.

"I am. It's nice to meet you." He removed his hat and extended his hand.

She was a stout woman with black hair streaked

with gray in a short, fluffy bob. Her long sleeve shirt was billowy and too thin for the Wyoming weather. The words *I'm here for the Wrangler butts* were printed over a backdrop of cowboy boots.

Aunt Brenda shoved his hand away and stood, wrapping him in a squishy hug. "Come here, boy. I'm so glad to meet you. Call me Aunt Brenda." She stepped back, examining him from head to toe. "You're even more handsome than Maddie let on."

Lucas cast a glance at Maddie who covered her face in shame.

Aunt Brenda shoved him into Maddie's side of the booth. "We've already ordered, but you can get something when the waitress comes back."

"I'm fine. I ate before I came." He knew Maddie had too, and he wondered if Aunt Brenda had pressured her into eating again.

The waitress appeared, propping her hand on the table while sticking her hip out. "What can I get you?"

Lucas started to wave her off, but Aunt Brenda broke in.

"He'll have a Diet Coke."

Unsure what to add to the order, Lucas shrugged. He wasn't about to saddle up against Aunt Brenda. "I guess I'll have a Diet Coke."

He wasn't sure he'd ever tried Diet Coke before. Water had always done him fine, but there was a first time for everything.

When the waitress disappeared to get his soft drink, Brenda leaned over the table. "So, who is a worthy dance partner for a young woman in this place?"

Maddie gasped. "I'm not dancing."

"I'm not talking about you. I need someone to sweep me off my feet tonight."

Delighted by Brenda's penchant for fun, Lucas leaned over the table and tilted his head toward the bar. "You see that man in the white shirt?" Lucas asked, indicating a robust bearded man with a round shape.

"The teddy bear?" Brenda asked.

"Yeah. That's Russell. He's your man."

Brenda narrowed her eyes at Lucas and asked, "Can he twirl me around like some of those rag dolls?" She pointed to the dancers currently on the floor.

"Yes, ma'am. He knows all the moves."

Aunt Brenda studied Russell. "I like 'em big."

Maddie groaned like an embarrassed teenager. "Aunt Brenda."

Brenda scooted from the bench seat of their booth and waved. "See you two later."

Maddie said, "Look at her. She's walking like a runway model instead of a fifty-five-year-old woman."

Sure enough, Brenda sauntered over to Russell and leaned on the bar beside him. Within seconds, his round face turned a shade of pink that might indicate cardiac issues rather than embarrassment.

"Don't worry. Russell needs a little spice in his life."

"You don't think she's too spicy for him?" Maddie asked.

"Is there such a thing?"

Maddie squinted. "I'm not really a spicy person, so I would say yes, there is such a thing as too spicy."

"You don't seem to mind that Brenda doesn't have a filter." She seemed like the opposite of Maddie in so many ways, but he could see the love between them.

"She has the best heart," Maddie explained.

"I like her. Maybe I should ask her to dance."

Maddie shoved his shoulder. "Don't you dare."

"What? Are you afraid we'll run away together?"

"No, but don't encourage her."

Lucas hooked his pinky with hers. "Will you dance with me?"

She ran her fingers over her ear, brushing back the hair that was usually restrained by her braid. "I already danced with you."

"That was weeks ago. Don't your feet itch to dance when you hear this song?"

The words of "Dirt on My Boots" by Jon Pardi pulsed through the room, igniting a fire in his blood.

Maddie eyed the dancers moving to the beat, then lifted her chin. "Okay. Let's dance."

Lucas whooped and scooted out of the booth. He offered his hand to her as she stood. The mass of people laughing and enjoying the night radiated energy around them. When they reached an open space, he twirled her to him.

Her smile grew as they danced, and he watched her face light up in excitement. Seeing her happy was the highlight of his days.

The song faded and they slowed to rest until the next one started up. She ran her fingers over her temples and through her long hair, and he itched to follow her hands and do the same.

Just as the next song started, Jameson stepped up beside them.

Lucas's first reaction was to frown, but Maddie's smile didn't fade.

"Hey." Her greeting was more bubbly than usual, making him wonder if the giddiness was left over from their dance or Jameson's presence.

"Can I cut in?" Jameson asked.

Maddie turned to Lucas as if asking him what she should do. They hadn't told anyone they were slowly working toward dating yet, so he was trying to give Jameson the benefit of the doubt.

"You don't need his permission to dance with me," Jameson said.

There it went. Benefit of the doubt, out the window.

Before Maddie could respond, Aunt Brenda

bumped into Lucas and Maddie from the other side. "Can I cut in?" It was more of an order than a suggestion as she dragged Lucas to another part of the room.

Lucas kept his eyes on Maddie and Jameson as they moved. Occasionally, he had to stretch his neck to see over or around the other patrons.

"Give her a chance to stand up for you," Brenda said. "She needs to fight for something she cares about every now and again."

Lucas whipped his gaze to Brenda. "What?"

"She'll tell him she's with you, and it'll hold a lot more weight than you flexing your muscles and puffing out your chest." Brenda ran her hands up and down his arms, indicating the muscles she referenced.

Lucas nodded. "Okay."

"Trust me. I know my girl. She has a loyal heart, and when she latches on, she doesn't waver."

He believed her. He'd seen Maddie's determination before, and he calmed knowing he was on the winning end of her devotion.

When the song was over, Maddie left Jameson with a friendly wave and sprinted straight into Lucas's waiting arms.

CHAPTER 21

MADDIE

"One more time, girl. I know you can do it."

Dolly shook her head, and a puff of air formed a cloud around her snout in the cold October morning.

Maddie had set up barrels in a cloverleaf pattern in one of the pastures the week before, and she and Dolly were taking full advantage. While the cutting horses got their exercise herding cattle, Dolly preferred the race.

The horse moved into her gallop, and Maddie's heart pounded as the wind cut at her face. Flutters filled her stomach as she leaned forward in the saddle. The smell of dry dirt and leather filled her head as the thrill of a smooth ride coursed through her.

Coming to a stop at the pasture entrance, she

patted Dolly's mane. "That's my girl. Let's go check on the others."

Minutes later, Maddie stepped into the stables and closed the door against the biting cold. Raised voices greeted her instead of the usual silence.

"I locked that gate," Lucas said. "I've never left a gate unlocked."

Jameson asked, "Then who was it?"

"Do you know how many times we go in and out of that gate every day? This is about Maddie, isn't it? You can't stand it that we're together."

Jameson huffed. "She'll wise up. I'm not too worried about it."

"It's not like you're really interested in dating. You're with a different woman every weekend."

"What do you care if the tourists want to have some fun?"

"That's not for Maddie!" Lucas yelled.

Maddie stepped up, interrupting the quarreling men. "Excuse me."

Lucas and Jameson whipped around like deer caught in headlights.

"That's enough," Maddie said. "Jameson, I told you I'm with Lucas. I know the two of you haven't lost any love here, but can't you be reasonable?" She crossed her arms over her chest. "Did you find the cattle?"

Jameson cleared his throat and shoved his hands into his pockets. "Well, we didn't actually lose any."

"So, no harm, no foul?" Maddie asked.

Jameson reluctantly agreed, "I guess you're right."

Maddie looked around the stables. "You need anything else here?"

Jameson cast a glance at Lucas. "I guess not."

Maddie tipped her hat. "See you at lunch. I need a word alone with Lucas if that's all right with you."

Jameson left without looking back, and Maddie waited until she heard the door close before addressing Lucas.

"What's going on between you two?"

"Would you believe me if I said he started it?"

She sighed.

Lucas stepped to her and wrapped her in his arms. "I'm joking. A little. It isn't anything we haven't done before and not anything to write home about."

Home. Where would she send a letter if she ever had to write home? The thought chilled her frustrations with the feuding men.

If Lucas didn't take the argument seriously, maybe she was reading more into it than she should. Her disappointment faded into hope. If the two men could brush it off at lunch, perhaps she should take a page out of their book and learn to let things go.

"He's just a little jealous," Lucas explained. "Jameson isn't a bad guy. He's actually someone you want to have on your side if things go south. He's just too worried about his jobs to commit to anyone."

Maddie nodded. "I know. I just don't like seeing you two at odds."

Lucas laughed and stroked her hair. "Get used to it. We've been throwing jabs since grade school, but it always passes, and we move on. I'm sorry about what I said. I don't think it was about you. We just rile each other up, and I got carried away."

"Good." Caring about Lucas's relationships with others was a step she hadn't taken with anyone else in her life. Other than Aunt Brenda, she had kept a safe distance from everyone. Now, she found that it was easy to care about someone else's daily struggles. Lucas was the exception to every rule she'd lived by until now, and stepping out of her comfort zone wasn't always a bad thing.

If Lucas could forgive and forget with Jameson on a daily basis, maybe there was hope that he would forgive her when he found out about her parents.

Maddie raised her head from his chest. "I love that you can overcome your disagreements with Jameson. It's one of the best things about you." If she was in his position, and someone asked her to forgive, could she do it?

Lucas tightened his arms around her waist, snuggling her close in the cool stable. "There's too much good in life to spend my time mad at someone. I have my family, two jobs, horses that are my best friends, and a woman beside me that I thank the Lord for every day. I'm too blessed to let disagreements ruin that."

Maddie cast her gaze at the dirt floor thinking about how Lucas spent his days saving people from danger and taking care of horses as if they were children. But she had never known anyone like that since she came from people who took from others without looking back. "There are still things about me that you don't know. I'm afraid to tell you because…"

"One day, you won't be afraid to tell me. You'll realize that I'll still be here no matter what. You won't lose me, Maddie. Whatever it is, we can get past it. I know your heart, and it's good." He ducked his head beneath her lowered chin, and she could see his sincerity. "If you've done something you know was wrong, you can ask God to forgive you. After that, you need to forgive yourself. People grow and change, and we all fall short."

Her lungs filled with an air that seemed to spread through her body, calming the fire in her veins.

"You're kind to everyone you meet. You love the horses and take care of them. You work hard and pray harder." Lucas's expression was serious. "You undervalue yourself, but I'm going to change that. Jesus didn't die for you so that you could wonder if you were worthy or good enough. I hope you realize that and never doubt yourself again."

His thumb brushed over her hairline on her forehead. "You're special. You're extremely special to me." His brows drew together as if his thoughts troubled him.

She felt it then, the shattering of the darkness around her heart that had kept her from knowing love for another person until now. She knew that what Lucas said was true, and it felt as if she *could* forgive. He didn't know it was her parents she needed to forgive, but Lucas's reminder that God calls us to forgive and love our neighbor sparked a new awareness in her.

"You're right. Thank you. I need to learn to forgive."

His beautiful smile held a challenge.

I dare you to love me.

It was a challenge she needed to accept. Because loving him was a risk, but it was a step she desperately needed to take. She needed to grow and learn, and Lucas was the man she wanted standing beside her when she did.

CHAPTER 22

MADDIE

A small-time rodeo was in town Friday night, and Maddie and Lucas skipped out early to be there for the kickoff. Maddie hadn't been to a rodeo in months, and the rush of anticipation crawled on her skin the entire drive to the arena.

The rodeo had been her escape during her teen years. Barrel racing with Dolly had been thrilling, and the few minutes of speed leading up to the push had kept her mind off any negativity she carried.

The cheering crowd, the strain of holding on, and the smell of dirt brought back memories of the happiest times in her life. Now, she was here in this space of comfort with Lucas, and every emotion was heightened.

She missed barrel racing, but it was equally thrilling to be holding Lucas's hand in a crowd of strangers. A rider finished her pattern, and the cheers roared around them. She stood, and Lucas was already there, sharing her elation at a sporting event she loved.

The way he looked at her had her heart racing at a pace that could compete with the horses. His smile was bright enough to rival the light of the stars, and he was looking at her.

That look was dangerous, but it was oh so welcome. It made her feel complete and loved in ways she never knew existed.

She wasn't strong enough to keep the distance between them. Did that make her weak? Was it wrong to give in to the happiness he made her feel?

It wasn't smart. Especially knowing his affections would be gone as soon as he found out about her parents. He'd more than likely drop her like a hot rock.

But when Lucas wrapped his arm around her shoulders and pulled her in to celebrate the sport she loved, she questioned everything she'd just imagined would happen. His smell was different tonight, and it was intoxicating. A smile tugged at her lips knowing he'd worn cologne for their night out together, even if it was to a smelly rodeo.

Lucas wrapped his arm tighter around her and rested his lips against her ear to whisper, "You're beautiful when you're excited about the things you love."

She chuckled as his hot breath tickled her ear.

Turning her body to him, she snuggled closer into his embrace. They were as close as two people could get, and she still wanted more.

She wanted to kiss him.

His gaze locked with hers, and there wasn't a hint of his usual playfulness. Instead, a fire burned there, restrained by the tension she felt in his arm around her.

A little while later, Lucas's eyes locked on her lips as he asked, "You want to get out of here?"

She nodded, and he linked their hands together as they stepped from the bleachers. The October night seemed colder as they jogged from the lights and crowds toward the parking area, but adrenaline coursed through her body, waking a happiness in her that had been sleeping for too long.

Lucas stopped at the edge of the parking field. The grass was nearly knee high, and it looked as if cars and trucks floated in a black ocean.

He crouched in front of her. "Hop on."

"What?"

"Get on my back. I'll carry you to the truck."

Laughing, she jumped on. He let out an exaggerated grunt, and she slapped his shoulder before wrapping her arms around his neck. "Cowboy up, big boy."

"You're the one wearing a shirt that says *Ride it like you stole it.*"

She threw her head back to the wide-open

Wyoming sky and laughed. The joy was so great, it refused to be contained within her, and she released it willingly in a way she'd never done before.

They reached his truck, and he set her on her feet beside the passenger side before turning quickly to open the door for her. His eyes were wide and glowing in the dim light pouring from the cab of the truck, no doubt mirroring her own.

When she didn't move to get in, he moved closer to her, his gaze tethered to hers by an invisible magnet.

He rested his hands on her waist and the pressure was easy at first but grew heavier by the second. His head dipped to hers until they were inches apart.

She flung her arms around his neck and slowly pulled him to her until his lips crashed into hers. There it was. The touch shocked her at first, and then it was too much to take in. It was a spark. It was light. And then it was an inferno. Her senses were overloaded.

The wind whipped around them, cheers roared in the distance, his cologne tingled in her nose, and that taste. Her mind finally focused on the feel of his soft lips brushing against hers, and the rest of the world faded away.

She should be drowning in panic. Instead, all she felt was Lucas anchoring her to this moment when everything was right.

The burning kiss turned into a series of sweet touches that left her paralyzed in his adoration. When his hands moved from her hips to cradle her face, he rested his forehead against hers.

"For once, I'm speechless," he confessed with a content huff of breath. "Give me a minute for my brain to catch up."

She rested one more peck on his lips and stepped into the truck. Lucas jogged around the front and hopped into the driver's seat. With the doors closed and the quiet cab surrounding them, they could have been the only two people in the world.

He didn't start the truck. Instead, he turned to her and whispered, "I don't want to go home."

"Me either."

He leaned over the bench seat and wrapped a gentle hand behind her neck and pulled her closer. He kissed her again, and she scooted closer to him. In the remote space that protected them, there was no hurry this time. The rush of adrenaline had been replaced by a caressing hunger that he filled with timeless kisses.

Between kisses, Lucas whispered, "I didn't know I was waiting for you, but I'm glad you're here now."

Maddie pinched her lips between her teeth before answering. "I'm glad I'm here with you. I had fun tonight too. Thank you for taking me."

He might not know how he'd lifted her up and given her a hope she'd been too scared to reach for in the past, but now, her heart begged to tell him everything. The kind, understanding man who wrapped her in his arms and whispered hope in her ear wouldn't turn her away.

At least, that was her prayer as he drove them home.

CHAPTER 23
MADDIE

Maddie didn't spend much time with Lucas the next week, but she didn't worry. He stopped by the stables as often as he could, and they were able to catch up at meal times. Every night, he either stopped by her cabin to tell her good night or made sure to call her if he was on his shift at the fire station.

There were times when his ranch duties were more demanding than others, so she focused on keeping the horses happy. She'd gained some new four-legged friends lately, as well as Camille and Asher who stopped by or called to chat regularly.

Lucas's truck rumbled to a stop at the stables in the early afternoon, and she jogged to meet him at the door.

"Hey, cowboy."

"Hey, pretty lady." He rested his hand on her hip

and leaned in for a quick kiss that left her dizzy. "Can you sneak away with me for a few hours?"

She craned her neck to see the six horses in the pasture. "Sure. Where are we going?"

"You like fishing?" he asked.

"I'm no expert, but I can bait a hook."

"That'll do. Hop in."

"Do you have rods?" she questioned.

Lucas pointed toward the bed of the truck. "Yep. We're all set."

She settled into the truck and let him lead her on a spontaneous midday adventure. Fishing was a quiet activity, but silence was rare around Lucas. He talked through everything he did, showing her the best spots, telling her where the fish would be, and pointing to a tree on the other side of the creek where he saw a mountain lion the last time he'd fished here.

After an hour of fishing Bluestone Creek, Lucas asked, "You want to move to Blackwater River?"

"Where is that?"

He pointed to the east. "Just that way. It intersects this creek a few yards up, but there's a clearing at the bank if we cut through."

She reeled in her line. "Sure. Lead the way." She took in the landmarks as they walked, familiarizing herself with the area. Blackwater Ranch was huge, and she hoped to know its reach one day.

"You remember when you gave me that grueling

interview when I first started working here?" she asked.

"Yeah."

"What made you ask those questions? About the pencil and the fruit?"

His mouth quirked to the side for a moment. "When I was in high school, we had a teacher who wanted to prepare us for college and the job force. We did mock interviews, and some of the questions were practical, but some were like the ones I asked you. I always thought those answers told more about the real person."

"So, if you were a fruit, what would you be?" she asked.

"Oh, a grape. Hands down."

"Why?"

"Because I like being around other people. Grapes grow in bunches."

Maddie nodded her understanding. "I get it. What about the pencil?"

"The eraser."

She grinned, remembering that her answer had been the lead. "Why the eraser?"

"Because it means I'd get a chance to make things right if I ever messed up. I like living in a world where forgiveness is real and within reach."

Forgiveness. That was a topic she needed to work on. She'd been praying about her feelings toward her parents, and maybe that meant she was ready to forgive them and stop letting their mistakes dictate her life.

It was fitting that she chose the lead and he chose the eraser. Together, they would make a complete pencil.

Lucas stopped at a thistle that reached to his thigh. "You know, you're a lot like a thistle."

She tilted her head and studied the purple plant. "An invasive species?"

He laughed and dug the heel of his boot into the ground at the roots. "No, I was thinking prickly and hardy."

She gasped in mock outrage. "How romantic. That's what every woman wants to hear." She shoved his shoulder and sprinted away from him.

He raced after her, and she held tight to her rod as she watched the ground for holes. A large mud pit, concealed by the tall grass loomed in her path, and she turned to stop him. Reaching out her arms between them, she cried, "Wait!"

It was too late. He barreled into her, and they both splashed into the thick mud. Her fishing rod fell from her outstretched hand, and Lucas landed on top of her. Dark mud was splattered on his face, and she laughed. "You have mud on your face."

"Oh really, Captain Obvious? You're *lying* in it." His nose scrunched up in distaste. "Also, I hope it's just mud. It smells awful."

She lifted her hands to cover her laugh, but they

were caked with mud. "Ugh!" She laughed some more, and Lucas watched her intently.

When she caught her breath, he swallowed hard and said, "I love it when you laugh."

The word *love* hung between them before settling into her middle. She loved *him*. He was the one showing her how to laugh again.

Before she made up her mind to say the words, he kissed her. She didn't care that she was stuck in the mud or that she tasted dirt. Her heart was riding off into the sunset with Lucas.

When he broke the kiss, he righted himself before helping her to her feet. The cold mud clung to her back, and she pulled off her flannel overshirt to reveal a T-shirt that read *Cowboy take me away.*

Lucas grabbed their rods in one hand and reached for her with the other. "I like your shirt."

"I thought it was fitting." She grabbed his hand and skipped to his side. "I need to get back to the truck. I'm going to freeze on the way home."

"It's not like I'm going to make you ride in the back. We're not far."

"I'm not getting in your truck like this."

"Oh, yes you are."

"I think I need to stop by the barn and hose off before going home for a shower."

Lucas cut his eyes at her and grinned. "You know why I said you're like a thistle?"

"We've been over this."

"You are prickly and hardy, but I was really thinking you're captivatingly beautiful. A bright color in a field of brown and green."

She breathed in his compliment and squeezed his hand. "Thank you."

The ride back to the cabins was short. Lucas turned up the heat in the cab and drove the paths of least resistance. They were both shivering in their boots by the time she jumped from the truck. "I'll catch you at dinner." She waved as he reversed the truck to head to his own cabin a few feet away.

Dixie met her on the porch, and she quickly scratched the dog's head. "Sorry, girl. I'm freezing and icky. I'll be back in a minute to play." Dixie came to Maddie's porch every evening after supper for fetch and snuggles.

Maddie stood at the doorway and watched Lucas enter his cabin. He was teaching her that finding her strength could be fun, and she was sure there were few things in life that were unpleasant with him by her side.

She called Lucas after her shower. The mere thought of going back out into the cold was enough to send a shiver up her spine.

He answered quickly. "Hey, you want to ride with me to supper?"

"Actually, I'm going to skip tonight. I'm still trying to warm up."

His voice took on a low, seductive tone. "I can help you with that."

She chuckled at his flirtation. "Thanks for the offer, but I think I'm going to turn in early. I'm tired." A yawn punctuated her sentence.

"Call me if you need anything."

Maddie ended the call and stepped into the small kitchen of her cabin to heat up some soup. She wasn't worried about hypothermia or anything, but she'd been seriously cold earlier after their romp in the mud, and she hadn't even warmed up after her hot shower.

Her phone rang just as she'd sat down to eat, and she hurried to answer when she saw that it was Aunt Brenda.

"Hey."

"Hey, sweetie. I didn't think you'd answer this time of day."

She stirred the steaming soup to cool it off. "I skipped supper with the family and decided on soup."

"The family? Have they adopted you as one of their own?" There was no animosity in her aunt's voice, only hopefulness.

"Maybe they have. I feel like I'm a part of something here."

"That's what I always hoped you'd find, baby.

I've been praying to the good Lord you'd find a good man one day and he'd be able to give you the family you've always wanted."

Maddie rested her spoon back in the bowl. "You know you were all the family I needed."

"No, you need a herd of people loving on you, and that Lucas boy is good for you. I hear it in your voice every time you call me. He's making you happy. So is that place. It's good for you."

"It is. I love it here." She paused, thankful she hadn't eaten yet. "I have to tell him. About Mom and Dad."

Brenda grunted a confirmation. "I don't know why you're so scared. That boy loves you."

Maddie squeezed her eyes closed. She hoped he loved her because her fragile heart was falling in love with him. "I just want him to know what he's getting into. He should know the dark parts of my past."

He should know the inner workings of her heart as well, but she needed to take one step at a time. See if he could handle the bad before she jumped in with the good.

In the last few weeks, he'd given her a million silent affirmations of his feelings. He would stroke her hand or hip as he passed her at meals, he teased kisses each time they were alone in the stable, and he always came by to tell her good night in person. She had no doubt his truck would park in front of his cabin after supper and he'd walk over to knock on her door tonight.

"Right now, it's just you, Lucas, and your fear. Wouldn't it be easier if it were you, Lucas, and God?"

Brenda was right. Maddie needed to ask God to guide her through the truth telling.

"I don't know much about love," Brenda confessed, "but I imagine the best part is being comfortable enough with someone to be yourself. I hope you find that."

Maddie hoped so too. All that was left was to find out if she could do it.

CHAPTER 24
MADDIE

Lucas didn't come over to tell her good night until much later, and she'd almost fallen asleep. She'd taken up reading *Lonesome Dove* to pass the time in the evenings, and the tome put her to sleep more often than not.

Her anxiety spiked when she heard his truck outside, and she contemplated waiting for another day. At this rate, he would know something was wrong the moment he saw her, and she'd have to spill it.

He knocked softly, and she opened the door for him.

"Hey. Can you come in for a little bit?"

Lucas toed off his boots. "Sure. What's on your mind?"

She waited until he'd settled into the section of the couch he favored.

"Maddie, is everything okay?" He took her hands in his.

"Um, I have something to tell you, and it's hard for me." When they were both seated facing each other, Maddie felt the weight of what she was doing crash into her. Everything she cared about could be taken from her after this.

"I need to tell you about my parents," she began. "They worked here when I was young, and that's how I remembered you." She picked up his hand in hers and began rubbing her thumb over the back. "I had a crush on you back then."

"Was I too dense to notice?" he asked. "If only I could give my kid self a swift kick in the backside."

"It's not that." Her heart felt as if it would explode in her chest. "You see, my parents aren't really gone. They're in prison because they stole from people. A lot of people. And sometimes they used me to do it."

She kept her gaze focused on their hands, and she continued when he didn't speak. "They would get a job, make everyone trust them, and then they would steal anything they could—money, supplies, animals, jewelry. Then we'd pack up and leave in the night and move on to the next victim."

He still hadn't spoken, so she lifted her chin to drive the truth home. "They stole from your family, Lucas. I don't know what they stole or how much, but they threw me into the car in the middle of the night." Maddie covered her mouth, determined not to let emotion cloud the confession he needed to hear. "I've never been so heartbroken as that night we left Blackwater."

Lucas rested his hand on her shoulder. The weight was comforting and terrifying.

"I assume your family knows. They hired me, knowing my parents are criminals, and I don't know why."

Lucas finally broke his silence. "Why shouldn't they hire you? You're not your parents, even if they did manipulate you into doing their dirty work sometimes. You were a kid."

"They were arrested in Amarillo when I was ten. I don't think they cared what happened to me, but Aunt Brenda was there, and she took me in. Then we moved around a lot for her job, but she always put me first." Maddie wiped a tear on the back of her hand. "Even when she didn't have to."

"She loves you," Lucas whispered, squeezing her shoulder.

"I know. She just put so much of her own life aside for me, and that's not the life she chose for herself."

"Yes, it is," Lucas said. "She chose to raise you."

She squeezed her eyes shut and whispered, "I'm sorry." Every muscle in her body began to shake with the force of her regret.

She would lose him now, and the loss would be devastating.

"Please look at me."

Lifting her head to him, she saw understanding in his eyes.

"Let's get one thing straight. You have it in your head that you're not good enough, and you're wrong. The fact that you care about being a good person makes you more than enough. Anyone who knows you can see it. You're letting your parents' mistakes take your happiness."

Lucas moved closer to her on the couch and brushed a hand over her hair. She'd taken the braid out earlier, and it lay loose over her shoulders.

"And also forgetting one important thing," he continued. "You're a daughter of the King, and your parents might not have loved you like they should have, but your Heavenly Father always will."

A sob broke from her at his words. He wrapped his arms around her, and rocked her from side to side as her tears abated.

When she'd calmed, he whispered into her hair, "If your parents didn't care enough about you to stay out of trouble, then that isn't a problem with you. It's a problem with them. Some people can't see others because they're too wrapped up in themselves."

Everything clicked into place, and she understood. The way Lucas really looked at others and gave them his full attention was the epitome of self-lessness. He saw their struggles and their needs, and he met them. The difference between him and her parents was that he was hardwired to freely give parts of himself—his time, his care, and his strength —to help others when they needed it.

Maddie's parents were missing that part, and it shouldn't bother her so much that she was a necessary casualty to them.

Lucas was the one who mattered. He was good, and she prayed with everything she had that she could keep him in her life.

"Why aren't you mad?" she asked through a sniffle.

"Why would I be mad?" He lifted her head from his chest. "Maddie, I told you nothing could change the way I feel about you. Your parents' bad choices have nothing to do with you, and I won't blame you for something someone else did."

He rested his hand against her cheek, and she leaned into the warmth.

"I love you, Maddie. I've never said that to anyone. I haven't felt it before."

She wanted to cry again, but not sad tears. He had erased those terrible feelings and replaced them with the most powerful emotion—love.

Lucas always had the right words to say, but he'd saved the most important words of his life for her.

"You don't have to say it back, but there's one thing I want you to do before you decide if you love me or not. I want you to get rid of the fear that I'll leave you. Now that I know about your parents, everything makes sense. I'm not going anywhere, and I need you to believe that."

She did. She believed every word. Her life may have been safer when she hid away behind her mask, but it wasn't better. Lucas had opened her heart to happiness.

"I know you're tired and have a lot to think about. I'll let you get some rest." He stood and kissed the top of her head. "Good night. I love you."

She hadn't composed herself enough to tell him she loved him too, but she did. She would make sure he knew the next time she saw him.

Learning about her parents hadn't shaken his love for her. It only seemed to make it stronger.

She closed her eyes and said a prayer of thanks for sending Lucas into her life. The peace about her parents that she'd been praying for finally came, and it was because she listened to her heart and trusted Lucas.

Her parents weren't made to love her, Lucas was. God had used him to slowly mend her shattered heart, and now, she felt brand new.

CHAPTER 25

LUCAS

Lucas hadn't slept a wink after telling Maddie he loved her. He hadn't been brave enough to stick around while she decided how to respond to him, but when she didn't show up for breakfast, he took that as an answer.

He'd been furious when she told him what her parents had done. Knowing they'd left her was one thing, but finding out how they'd used her as a child was enough to boil his blood.

No wonder the happy little girl he vaguely remembered had grown into the guarded woman now invading his every thought. She was the kind of person who felt responsible for everything, and he prayed she would give herself grace.

He hadn't said much to anyone at breakfast. The only thing on his mind was Maddie and how scared she'd been to tell him about her parents' crimes.

Had they really stolen from the ranch? If they had, it might have gone unnoticed. His mom and dad had never mentioned it, but the news had spread like wildfire when Hunter's dad had run off with thousands of dollars. He had to believe the same would have happened with her parents.

It didn't matter. None of that mattered to him where Maddie was concerned. It wasn't her fault, and he loved her no matter what. He loved her more now that she had trusted him enough to share a private part of her past with him.

He didn't hang around after breakfast, but Asher stopped him before he could get past the front porch.

"Hey, where's Maddie today?"

"I'm not sure." Lucas settled his ivory cowboy hat on his head and looked toward the stables. "I'll catch up with you later."

"Nice talk. We should do this again sometime."

Distracted, Lucas tipped a finger to his brother in good-bye and made his way to the stables. The last thing he wanted was for things to change between him and Maddie. He should tell her that there wasn't any pressure to return his love. He'd wait for her, but a sickening thought settled in his gut. What if she never loved him? He would have to work beside her every day, knowing she didn't have feelings for him the way he did for her.

He rubbed a hand down his face as he parked

and got out of the truck. Whatever thoughts were going through her head, they'd both be better off if they just got everything out in the open.

The stables were quiet as he entered, but there were signs of Maddie. The stalls were clean, the tack was perfectly stored, and her truck was out front.

A sharp pain stabbed his chest again. How could her parents have left her? How could they choose to lose her? Lucas would give anything to be with her always and see her happy.

A barrel sat in the middle of the breezeway on the far side of the stables, and he moved to investigate. Was she setting up another barrel pattern in the pasture?

The barrel was topped with a square cut of plywood, and a plate sat atop it. On the plate sat three sandwiches with peanut butter and grape jelly oozing out around the crust. Lucas smiled as he read the message written in squirt jelly on each one.

An I, a heart, and a U.

Lucas eagerly scanned the stables for her, and his heart raced with the revelation.

She loved him too.

Maddie rested her shoulder against the doorframe of his office. Her arms were crossed over her chest, but a bright smile greeted him.

He closed the distance between them, and she was wrapped in his arms before she had a chance to say anything.

She didn't need to say anything. She'd shared her heart with him in a fun way that showed him that she saw his quirks and loved him anyway.

"I love you." Her words were a whisper in his ear as he twirled her in a circle.

"I love you too. I love you enough to make up for both of your parents." He placed her feet on the ground and stared into her sea-green eyes, over-come with happiness.

Maddie rested her hands on his cheeks. "You don't have to. What I feel for you has nothing to do with them. I don't feel like I'm missing out on anything when you're around."

He leaned in to kiss her, and the emotion in his heart combined with the tight hold she had on his shoulders sent him reeling. He was thankful the Lord had seen fit to send her back here after so many years. He was glad she'd found a home in the place he loved. He was happy to be holding the one woman who understood his drive, his playfulness, and his heart.

She deepened the kiss, and he obliged her by lifting her feet off the floor in his all-encompassing embrace.

When he put her back on the ground, she smiled. Her expression reflected the love he felt in his heart. "Did you eat breakfast?"

"Not really. I was too worried about you to stomach food."

She gestured to the sandwiches. "There are two for you, and one is for me."

Lucas raised his hand. "I call the one with the heart."

She rolled her eyes and shoved his shoulder toward the barrel. "They all taste the same."

"Says you. Hearts are special."

He hadn't expected Maddie, but she fit into his life perfectly. Hearts *were* special, and some needed more patience and understanding than others.

Maddie's heart was certainly worth the wait.

CHAPTER 26

MADDIE

Maddie tilted her head back to study the exposed beams. "It's going to be amazing. I can't wait until it's finished."

Noah and Camille's house was still under construction, but the walls were up. Maddie scanned each empty room as her friend pointed out her intentions and decorating ideas for the new construction.

"We'll have a full front porch looking out at the ranch. Oh, I haven't even shown you the best part. We'll have a garage! I'll actually get to park my car *inside*."

Maddie chuckled. "Wow. You're living the dream. I haven't lived this far north in years, and I'm not looking forward to scraping ice and snow off my windshield."

Camille's expression was full of pity. "I'm so

sorry. Fair warning. It's worse than you're anticipating."

"Thanks for the heads up."

Maddie's phone rang, and she reached into her
jacket pocket. An unknown number lit up on the
screen. "Let me answer this. I'm not sure who it is."

"Sure, I'll be in my fancy new garage if you need
me." Camille stepped through a doorway on the far
side of the room.

"Hello?"

The rough voice of a man asked, "Hi, is this
Maddie Faulkner?"

"Yes."

"My name is Rick Tessaro. I'm a paramedic in
Franklin, Tennessee. We just transported a Brenda
Phillips to Elton General Hospital, and you're listed
as her emergency contact."

"Yes, she's my aunt. Is she okay?" Adrenaline
raced through her system as she sprinted for the
door where Camille had just disappeared.

"She suffered a heart attack, and she's been
released from our care to the doctors and nurses at
Elton General. Any further information regarding
her condition would have to come from them."

"Thank you, Mr. Tessaro. I'm on my way."

Camille was waiting in the garage with a look of
concern painted on her face. "What's wrong?"

"It's my aunt. She's had a heart attack. I need to
get back to Tennessee." Maddie gripped at her

chest, wringing the material of her shirt and jacket. How could she get there fastest? A plane was the obvious choice, but she needed her truck. She'd just have to leave her truck here and drive Aunt Brenda's car.

That would mean leaving Dolly, but she didn't have time to drive across the country and make enough stops for the horse. She didn't have time to wait for the vet to give a Coggins test and approve the horse for travel.

Camille's concern broke through Maddie's racing thoughts. "Oh no. Did they say anything about her condition?"

"No. I'll have to call the hospital on my way." Maddie's chest ached, and she grabbed Camille's hand. "Can you drop me off at my cabin?"

"Of course. Let's go."

They ran to Camille's 4Runner and jumped in. Within seconds, they were speeding over the hills of the ranch toward home.

Home. The thought broke her heart. It wasn't home anymore. Not when Aunt Brenda needed her halfway across the country for who knew how long.

Please, God. Please keep my aunt safe. I need her.

"You need to call Lucas too. He'll want to know."

Maddie's chin jerked up, pulled from her thoughts by her friend's comment. "Of course." The words came out hollow, barely a whisper. She would have to tell Lucas, and the pain that had slashed her heart at the tragic news about her aunt had just magnified.

Within minutes, Camille was parking in front of Maddie's cabin. The colorful Christmas lights that lined the roof were twinkling in the early dusk.

"What can I do to help?" Camille asked.

Maddie rubbed a hand over her neck as she thought. "Can you run up to the main house and see if you can find a flight to Nashville? I don't have a computer here, and I need to pack."

"Are you packing up everything?"

"I don't know yet. I don't know how bad things are or how long she'll need me." There were so many unknowns. Maddie loved stability and sure things. The panic was beginning to set in, and she tried to steady the shake of her hand on the door handle.

"Oh, Maddie." Camille reached across the console to wrap her friend in a hug. "I hope everything is all right. Please keep me posted, and let me know if you need anything else. I'll check on that flight."

"Thanks, Millie. The sooner, the better. I need to leave tonight." Maddie took a deep breath and huffed it out in a rush before releasing her friend and darting from the vehicle. She had a lot of work to do, and she still had some phone calls to make.

She started with the hospital, and a nurse confirmed that Brenda was stable in the Cardiac Intensive Care Unit, but a triple bypass surgery would be necessary within the next few days. They were still running tests to see when Brenda would be strong and stable enough to endure the procedure. Maddie let her know she would be there before the surgery and asked the nurse to keep her number handy in case anything changed.

Camille called twenty minutes later with a flight leaving tonight. Maddie rattled off her information, and Camille booked the seat.

Maddie zipped her overnight bag and slung it over her shoulder. "Thank you for helping. This would have taken me so much longer without you."

"No problem. Have you told everyone?"

"Actually, I haven't told anyone. I made the call to the hospital, and then I've been packing ever since." She put Camille's call on speakerphone to text Lucas to meet her at her cabin. He could be anywhere on the ranch, and it might take him a while to wrap up what he was working on and get to her.

"I just asked him to meet me here. I'll go talk to his parents while I wait."

"Listen, I know this is really bad, but just remember that we're here for you."

"I know. Thank you."

Camille hung up as Maddie hopped into her truck and headed for the main house. Mama Harding was sweeping the front porch, and Maddie prayed for the words to say. This woman had taken her in like the mother she'd always wished for. Now, she would have to leave her, and the injustice was like a knife in her stomach.

Maddie ran to the woman and wrapped her in a hug. "Mama, I have to go."

"Oh, sweetie. I was afraid of that when Camille said she needed to book you a flight. When will you be back?"

Maddie whispered into Mama Harding's hair, "I don't know. It's my aunt, and she'll need me while she recovers. I don't know if she'll ever be able to make it without my help."

"We'll be praying for you both, and Dolly will have a home here as long as you need."

Maddie swallowed the emotion in her throat and squeezed her eyes closed. This couldn't be happening. She'd just found these people that she loved. How could she give up this family when it was everything she'd ever wanted?

Dixie brushed up against Maddie's legs and barked. She'd missed their play time this evening, and her furry friend was coming to collect, oblivious to the ripping of Maddie's heart.

She'd been searching for this place her whole life, and it would break her to leave it after knowing the good it held.

"I have to go. Thank you for everything. I'll send money for Dolly's care."

Mama Harding released her and patted her

shoulder. "We love you. Don't forget us. You're always welcome here."

Maddie nodded, afraid to trust her voice at first. "I love you too."

She broke then. Her fragile heart she'd failed to protect shattered into pieces she wasn't sure she could collect again.

Covering her mouth to contain the emotion, she rushed from the porch and back into the safety of her truck.

Her sobs were uninhibited in the quiet space, and she let them free. She would have to tell Lucas now, and that would be hardest. She needed to be on the road soon, but the worst of the night was waiting for her.

CHAPTER 27
MADDIE

Before she could face Lucas, she needed to say her good-byes to Dolly. Maddie hadn't been more than twenty-five miles from her horse in the last seven years, and the distance would be tough on both of them.

She parked near the fence that lined the south pasture and set out to find the mare. Dolly was munching grass along the eastern fence, and she came over when she spotted Maddie.

"Hey, sweet girl." The other words she had for the horse were stuck in her throat, and she used the time they had left to breathe in the smell and comfort of her friend.

"We'll be together soon. I don't know when, but I'll make sure of it." She wasn't sure how she would afford boarding for Dolly in Franklin without a job, but Mama Harding had offered to keep her. That was one weight off her shoulder for the moment.

Maddie cleared her throat and patted Dolly one last time. "I love you. Don't forget me."

Dolly huffed and extended her neck as Maddie stepped away, but there wasn't any time left. She needed to get on the road. Aunt Brenda was waiting for her, alone and tired in a hospital room.

Maddie drew on the comfort she'd just gained from Dolly as she pulled the truck up beside Lucas's at her cabin. He sat in one of the rocking chairs on her front porch and stood to meet her at the truck.

"Hey, is everything okay?"

Maddie wrapped her arms around his waist and cried on his chest. "No, everything is wrong. Brenda had a heart attack, and she's all alone."

Lucas's warm arms embraced her, holding together the pieces that were falling apart. "I'm sorry, Maddie. Is she okay?"

The concern in his voice reminded her of the severity of her aunt's condition. "She'll need surgery as soon as she's stable enough. I have to go to her."

"I'll go with you. Let me pack a bag."

"No," Maddie pulled away from him. "You can't. I have to fly out tonight, and you have to be at the fire station in the morning. I don't know when I'll be back, and she's going to need me during her recovery. I'm the only one she has."

Lucas held out his hands as if he didn't understand. "I'll call Travis to fill in for me. You shouldn't be alone right now."

"Listen to me," her husky voice was raw in her sadness. "You can't come. I don't know if I'm coming back."

He stared at her, and the cowardly part of her was thankful she couldn't see his eyes well in the growing dark.

"The ranch needs you. You have another job too. You can't just run off with me."

"Of course I can, and I will." His resolve was a stone dropped between them.

"That's crazy. You have responsibilities here. Your life is here."

He grabbed her hand and squeezed as if she might float away from him if he let go. "No, you're my life. You need me, and that's all that matters. I can help."

Maddie made a point to pronounce her words. "Too many people need you here."

"Why don't you want me to come with you?" he begged.

"I just told you! They need you here."

"You need me too. Do you think they're worth more than you are? Because that's not true."

Of course she knew that. She'd never doubted her worth in the eyes of the Lord, but with people,

she was still learning how she fit into the grand
scheme of things.

But Lucas was right. He had never undervalued
her, and he'd built up her confidence and self-worth
day after day. Leaving him like this felt like strap-
ping him with the same tragedy she feared in her
own life—being left by someone she loved.

"I know that, but I don't know enough yet. I'll let
you know everything that's happening."

"So, we'll just have a long-distance relationship
for a while. Right?"

How could she agree to continue their relationship when she wasn't sure she'd be able to come
back at all? Everything was so uncertain, and panic
rose in her throat.

"Maddie, we can still be together, can't we?"

She pulled her hand from his and covered her
mouth. Stepping away from him, she forced herself
to breathe. In and out. In and out.

"Please don't do this," he begged.

"I'm not trying to do anything. I can't help it
that my aunt needs me on the other side of the
country! I don't want to leave, but I have to go." Her
words were fractured and full of the hysteria filling
her thoughts.

"You broke me," Lucas said, and his voice
cracked on the last word.

"What?"

"You know what I mean. I've lived a happy, simple life. I'd never experienced real heartbreak or pain before you. Then you told me about your parents, and it tore me up."

He stepped closer to her but didn't reach to touch her. "You broke me. Horses break when they realize they're better off taming the wild side in exchange for someone who loves and cares for them. That's what you did to me. You changed me. You made me see a side of you—a side of the world—I'd never experienced before, and I bonded to you."

She could feel the hurt in his voice. What had she done? She'd done this to both of them when she opened her heart and let him in.

He touched her wet cheek with his fingertips, and she wanted to scrub the traitorous tears away. Instead, she was stuck, unable to move under the weight of their combined sadness.

"Please don't leave. Not forever. Just say you'll be back, or say you'll let me come to you later when things settle down."

Maddie slowly shook her head, and his fingers slid down her cheek and back to his side.

"I can't promise you anything. I want to say I know this will be over soon, and I'll be back, but I don't know anything right now."

Lucas nodded and brushed his hand over his mouth. The scrub against his five o'clock shadow created a bristling sound that punctuated the silence around them.

"Will you call me? Please let me know if you make it okay?"

She nodded. "I can do that."

"Will you answer when I call after that?"

Her heart shattered. Her chest felt wide open and raw. "Yeah," she whispered into the darkness.

He wrapped his arms around her and kissed her hard on the top of her head. "Go." He released her in a quick movement and stepped back.

The thud of her heart was loud as she walked away from him. Her lungs felt heavy, and every muscle in her body protested the direction she'd chosen.

Lucas called out to her as she opened the door of her truck.

"Maddie."

He stood where she'd left him, strong and solid like the Rockies.

"I love you. I'll love you for the rest of my life."

His declaration was bold and full of truth, and she let it wrap around her like a blanket on a cold night.

She wiped her face with the sleeve of her jacket and said, "I love you too."

When the truck door slammed and she started the engine, the bright headlights illuminated the man she loved—the one she had to drive away from tonight. It felt so much like the last time she'd left this place, and the memory crushed her.

Tonight, she'd broken her own heart as well as Lucas Harding's.

CHAPTER 28

LUCAS

The next week hadn't brought much news from Maddie. Her texts were short updates about her aunt, and she'd only answered one of his calls. Early mornings and late nights were hardest without her. In the middle of the day, he could round up enough work to keep his mind busy, but in the quiet moments, he couldn't help but think of her and worry.

He'd made it to the couch in the living room this morning before the weight of her absence set in. He was lying on his back with an arm draped over his eyes when a knock sounded at the cabin door.

"It's open!"

He uncovered his eyes as the door creaked open. Camille stood in the doorway, framed by the early-morning sun.

"Hey, how you doing this morning?" she asked tentatively, as if she might scare him off.

He let his arm fall back over his eyes. "I'm fine. Just getting a late start. What are you doing here so early?"

"They're putting in the windows at the house today. I got excited and came to watch." She eyed the tiny kitchen and asked, "You want me to brew up some coffee?"

"Nah, thanks though. I think I'll just sit here and mope a little more."

Camille chuckled and sat down on the coffee table beside the couch. "I thought the cowboy was supposed to do the leaving."

"Ha-ha. She has jokes."

"Too soon?"

Lucas didn't answer. He'd never been one to put down someone else's attempt at humor, but he wasn't feeling cheery today.

Camille sighed. "Maybe you need to get up and do something."

Lucas lifted his arm so he could narrow his eyes at her. "I worked all night. I've tried that. Hence my reluctance to greet the day with bells on."

"Oh." She wrapped her jacket tighter around her middle and crossed her arms. "Are you coming to breakfast?"

Lucas sat up and stretched. "I think I'll just hang

around here for a bit before I have to meet Asher at the stables."

"Suit yourself, but don't hole up in here by yourself all the time."

"I'll be at lunch and supper," he promised.

Camille left without any more prodding, and Lucas threw himself into work. The colder weather brought with it dozens of new chores and repairs around the ranch, and he looked forward to meal times just so he could thaw his bones.

After supper, his mom laid a gentle hand on his shoulder. "Can you help me clean up?"

"Of course." Lucas stood and began gathering empty plates without further comment. He was elbow deep in soapy water in the kitchen before his mother propped her hip against the counter next to him.

"You doing okay?"

He nodded and smiled for his mom. "I'm okay. Just tired. I worked on the skid steer pretty late last night."

His mother crossed her arms. "Have you heard from her?"

"Nah. She's busy. She said Brenda made it through surgery, but she's real weak."

"What about Maddie? How is she holding up?"

Lucas shrugged and kept his hands moving in the soapy water. Keep moving. If he was working, he wasn't thinking. "She hasn't really said."

His mom brushed her hands on her apron. "We all love her. She could still come back."

"Maybe." There was a chance, but it wasn't one that looked too promising right about now. "I didn't get to keep her long enough," he whispered.

"None of us did." She rubbed a hand over his back and gave him a towel to dry his hands.

With the chore complete, Lucas felt lost again. If he'd done a better job of showing her how much she meant to him, maybe she would be returning his calls. He'd tried his best to be everything her parents weren't for her.

"What were her parents like?" he asked.

Mama thought for a moment before answering. "They were quiet. Kept to themselves. I could tell they were hard on Maddie, but they didn't seem cruel. Why? Did she say something about them?"

"Why did they leave the ranch?"

She huffed a big sigh before speaking. "Your Uncle Butch ran them off."

"What? How?"

"They left about a year before Butch stole the money from us. He was crafty, and he didn't just decide to rob us blind on a whim. He'd been planning for years, and they were getting in his way."

"So, they didn't steal anything?" Lucas questioned.

"Not that we're aware of, and your dad is very particular about the finances around here."

"Maddie thinks they left because they stole from us. They used to make her do some of the sneaking around. She said they hopped around the country stealing from their employers."

His mother raised a hand to her mouth. "Oh, that's terrible. No one should use their kids like that."

"It's a wonder she ever trusted any of us." Lucas scrubbed a hand over his jaw and yawned.

"I know. You need to hit the hay. Go on. We're finished here."

"See you in the morning." He stopped at the door and said, "And thank you for being a good mom. I really appreciate you."

Her dark eyes mirrored his own as she smiled. "Love you, son. Don't give up on her."

"I love you too."

He couldn't give up on her. It wasn't in his blood to throw in the towel, and Maddie was worth fighting for. He had an idea, but he needed Brenda's address.

CHAPTER 29

MADDIE

"We need to leave in two!" Maddie shouted through the house.

Brenda shuffled into the living room and grunted. "Hold your horses. I'm coming."

Maddie refused to dwell on her aunt's mention of horses. One thought would be enough to start a landslide that would ruin her mood for the rest of the day. "I just don't want to be late."

"I know you put a lot of stock in these follow-up appointments, but I don't need a doctor to tell me how I feel. I'm fine."

Brenda's usual bright attitude had been sharp lately, and Maddie knew her own anxious disposition was to blame. Concern for her aunt's condition had consumed her every thought. She'd gone through an entire prayer journal in the last month. There were other things she could think about, but it was easier to train her focus to one of the many things she couldn't control.

They loaded into the car without further comment. Three hours and a good report from the cardiologist later, Brenda's one-month post-surgery appointment was behind them.

As soon as they parked on the curb at the house, Brenda pointed toward the front door. "Your delivery came while we were gone."

Lucas had been sending Maddie a rose and a note every other day for weeks now. They still called and texted, but the conversation between them was strained. Until she had some idea of what their future might hold or if they even had a future, she was reluctant to open her heart again.

She picked up the flower on her way inside and ripped into the note. Telling herself she should temper her feelings for Lucas was one thing, but the distance and his love notes only amplified her feelings.

Setting the rose on the table next to the vase of flowers he'd already sent, she read the note.

I'll love you until the last one dies.

She studied the vase of roses in varying degrees of decline. Some had already been thrown out, but others were vibrant and blooming.

It wouldn't be long until the most recent rose would see its last day. Would he continue to send new flowers?

She picked up the new rose to add it to the vase and stopped. A smile spread across her face as her eyes tingled with the first signs of tears. It was made of plastic. He'd sent her a flower that would never die.

Until now, she'd been content to live her life alone. But when Lucas Harding opened her heart, she hadn't known love or the heartache that comes with it. If he hadn't been so welcoming with his love and kindness, maybe if he hadn't been so charming and sweet, she would've been able to resist him and protect her heart.

Brenda stepped up behind her and said, "You've done enough running. Why don't you go home?"

Maddie picked up the stack of notes Lucas had sent. "I can't do that. You need me here."

Her aunt shook her head and pursed her lips. "How many times do I have to tell you that I'm fine?"

"At least a hundred more," Maddie said without looking up.

Brenda rested her hands on her hips. "Fear keeps us from opening our hearts to love. I don't want that for you."

"I'm not afraid. You just need me here, and I'm not leaving you."

Maddie flipped through the notes and read one from last week.

You have all of me. You'll always be my Maddie.

She bit the inside of her lip and dropped the note onto the table. Here he was claiming her in his heart when he had no obligation to her. He'd promised to love her when her own parents hadn't.

Brenda fidgeted and folded her arms across her chest. "You *are* scared. You're stuck in your fear because it's all you've known, but I'm here to tell you that God has something better planned for you. You let your parents' mistakes rule your life. Don't drown yourself because of them. Be proud of yourself."

Maybe Maddie *was* afraid. She often questioned if she should have told Lucas he could come visit when he asked, but she was afraid to let herself have that hope.

The first note he'd sent struck her as a sign.

When you left, I wasn't finished. I won't ever be finished loving you. I have things left to say to you, and a lifetime left to love you. I'll love you for life.

"What can I do? I don't know when I'll be able to go back, so what could I even tell him?"

Brenda scoffed. "Don't give me that. You can go back now, but you're using me as an excuse. And, well, I'm tired of it. Just because things didn't work out the way you planned doesn't mean it's over. You're going to have to fight for it."

Maddie dropped the notes and faced her aunt. "You dropped everything in your life for me, and I won't leave you when you need me. You're the only person who has ever cared about me, and—"

"And now I'm not the only one. Lucas cares about you, and he needs you too."

"Not like you do! You had a heart attack!"

Brenda waved her hand in the air. "That was a month ago. You heard the doctor today. I'm healthy as a horse."

"Are you making horse references on purpose?" Maddie asked.

"Maybe. What's it to you?"

"Why are you trying to confuse me? I just care about you, and I won't leave you when you need me."

Brenda covered her face and sighed. "You're impossible. If you won't go, then I'll go."

"What?" Maddie's volume rose.

"I'm moving to Blackwater. I've been talking to a realtor this week, and I'm going to make an offer on a house tomorrow."

The only thing Maddie could hear was her own breath. "Why didn't you tell me?"

"Because I wanted you to go on your own. I wanted you to be brave and trust that I can do this on my own. I'm really okay now, but if it makes you feel better to have me closer, I'll just go with you."

"No." Maddie shook her head. "You can't move halfway across the country because of me."

"It's not only because of you. I enjoyed myself

when I visited you, and I think it's time I settled down. I need a quieter life." Brenda stepped closer and turned Maddie's cheek. Her voice was softer now. "I know nobody ever taught you how to stick around, but now is the time to learn. I don't mean for me. I mean for your future."

Brenda rolled her eyes and gave an exaggerated sigh. "And for Pete's sake, you need to call that man and tell him you're coming home."

Maddie smiled and pulled her phone from her pocket.

"Or better yet," Brenda said, "you could tell him in person."

Maddie cocked an eyebrow at her aunt's suggestion.

"Fly out there this weekend. See Dolly, tell Lucas you love him, and get your job back."

Could she really have all those things as well as her aunt Brenda? It was too good to be true.

"Thank you," Maddie whispered.

"On to the next adventure," Brenda said. The same words she'd used at every move throughout their lives together.

Maddie wrapped her arms around her aunt. "I love you."

Love was all around her lately, and there was someone else she needed to tell.

CHAPTER 30
MADDIE

Three days later, Maddie gripped the armrest of her plane seat and squeezed her eyes closed. She'd never been a fan of flying, much less flying alone. The plane jerked as it hit the runway and bounced again as it settled in. She held her breath as the huge flying machine somehow decelerated from hundreds of miles per hour to a gentle coast in a few seconds' time.

Finally releasing the breath she'd been holding, she opened her eyes to a brown landscape. Thankfully, she'd arrived on a day with no snow. She hated having to ask Camille to pick her up at the airport, and driving in the snow would have been worse.

Fifteen minutes later, Maddie stepped into baggage claim. Camille leaned against a pole near the exit, and they spotted each other simultaneously.

Camille sprinted to greet her with open arms. "I'm so glad you're back." Her grip on Maddie's neck tightened with her words.

"You and me both. I missed you."

Camille leaned back and brushed her long, dark hair from her shoulder. "I wanted to tell Lucas so bad."

"I'm glad you didn't. I want it to be a surprise."

The carousel sounded an alarm and began moving. "Did you have a bag?" Camille asked.

"Nope. I can't stay long this time, but hopefully I'll be back for good soon."

Camille extended her bent elbow to Maddie with a smile. "Then let's get you home."

M addie ran an anxious hand down her braid and paced next to Dolly's stall. "Why am I so nervous?" She shook out her sweaty hands before rubbing them on the front of her jeans.

An excited bark drew her attention to the door of the stable, and Dixie came bounding around the corner. The border collie barged into her, and she had to balance herself. "Easy, girl."

Maddie stopped petting the dog when Lucas entered the stables. He stopped at the door, staring at her with an expression she couldn't read. She needed something to go on. Was he angry? Hurt? Glad to see her? She couldn't tell.

She stepped away from Dixie and took a few timid steps toward him. She'd played this speech over and over in her head on the way here, but now, her mind was blank.

"I got homesick," she whispered.

When he didn't move or respond, she clarified. "*You* are my home."

Lucas erased the few feet between them and wrapped her in his arms. His embrace was warm and everything she'd dreamed it would be.

Of course he would welcome her with open arms full of grace. Her Lucas possessed kindness and understanding above anything she'd ever experienced. He'd accepted her from the start, and he'd promised her he would hold to it.

She could trust him. She would always trust him.

Maddie sniffed. "I realized that when I went back to Tennessee, I did the one thing I have always hated. I left." She nuzzled her face into his shoulder. "I know love shouldn't leave, but scared love is different. I'm not trying to justify what I did. I was wrong, and I'm so sorry."

Lucas rubbed his strong hand over her hair and shushed her. "You should have gone, but I just didn't want that to mean we were finished. I love you so much it filled my every thought. When you were gone, all that was left was a void. Do you know how hard it is to feel whole again after something like that?"

Maddie nodded slowly. She did know.

"I have something to tell you," Lucas said. "Your parents never took anything from the ranch."

Maddie raised her head. "What?"

"I talked to my mom. She said my uncle ran them off. They never got a chance to take anything."

The words were so simple but so heavy at the same time. The crippling guilt she'd felt since she arrived had been for nothing.

"Thank you for telling me." She wrapped her arms around his neck and buried her face in his shoulder.

"You needed to know that none of that was ever your fault."

"I love you," Maddie blurted, "and what we had was special and precious, and I should've fought to keep it instead of running scared. It hurt me to leave as much as it hurt you. I'm sorry I hurt *us*."

"I know you're scared," Lucas whispered, "but the only thing that scares me is living a life without you by my side." He swallowed hard and squeezed her. "I'm so glad you're home."

Home. She was finally home, and the realization brought tears to her eyes. She was home, here with Lucas. Being away from him only solidified her feelings.

"I love you," she said as she wiped her cheeks.

"I've loved you all along. I was just afraid to admit it to myself. I was afraid it would hurt too much when you didn't love me back."

Lucas laughed. "As if I could stop myself from loving you back. You were made for me. And, Maddie." He stroked her damp cheek and smiled. "I'll love you for life."

She leaned her cheek against his strong chest and held him close. "Let's go see if I can get my job back."

EPILOGUE

Asher tugged the gray wig onto his head. "I'm kind of jealous."

Camille snatched the half apron from him. "Find you a Mrs. Claus, and you can be Santa next year. Give me that wig, and don't mess it up."

He handed over the hair piece, and Maddie rested the wig onto her blonde hair while Camille pinned it into place.

Lucas and Maddie had volunteered to be Santa Claus and Mrs. Claus for the Blackwater Christmas parade next week. It was a treat seeing Maddie smiling and putting herself out there after she spent so much time hiding. Asher had worried about her fitting in when she first came to the ranch, but she'd opened up to them on her own. Well, he imagined it was Lucas who had coaxed her out of that tough shell.

"She looks like Granny Harding!" Asher bent at the waist, laughing. "Put on the glasses." He pointed toward the various accessories sitting on the table in the meeting room.

Maddie adjusted her gray wig and added the thin-rimmed glasses. "How do I look?"

With her Mrs. Claus costume complete, she was barely recognizable as the twenty-three-year-old horse hand. Mama Harding draped a fuzzy white shawl over Maddie's shoulders while Camille tucked stray gray hairs into the red velvet cap.

"I can't believe you're doing this. Photos or it didn't happen." Asher pulled his cell phone from the back pocket of his jeans.

Maddie snapped her fingers and fixed him with an icy glare that could rival the winter wind. "Put it down, and no one gets hurt."

"Oh come on. Everyone in town is gonna see you soon," Asher whined.

Maddie raised her brows, daring him to contradict her. "It's a surprise."

"This is the best Christmas surprise ever," Camille said. "Lucas is going to lose his mind when he sees you."

Asher glanced over his shoulder at the door. "Where is he? How long does it take to put on a Santa costume?"

"Maybe he needed help," Maddie said. "You saw how many pieces my costume had."

Asher bumped Maddie's shoulder playfully. He was glad she was here. She'd been forced to leave twice, and anyone with eyes could see that the ranch was her home. Plus, Maddie needed a family—people to love and love her back—and she had that here.

"I'll go check on him." Asher stood to find his brother, but the main door to the meeting room opened, and in stepped a rotund Santa.

"Ho Ho Ho, Merry Christmas!" Lucas bellowed as he dramatically threw his arms out in greeting. His white beard hung to his chest and a puffy belly preceded him into the room.

Maddie clapped and bounced on her toes. "You look amazing!"

Lucas left his arms open for Maddie to run into them. The happy couple embraced as Camille started throwing her hands around.

"Watch her wig! Don't mess up the hair."

"Let me have this moment with my old lady!" Lucas shouted.

Maddie chuckled as her boyfriend nuzzled into her neck. "You're gonna be a beautiful grandma one day. I'm so glad I picked you."

Asher slapped a hand on Lucas's shoulder as he passed. "As if you had women lining up to pick from. Be glad Maddie picked *you*."

Lucas's gaze was focused on Maddie. "Trust me. I'm aware."

An unsettling twist gripped Asher's gut, stealing his good mood. He was used to being the happiest guy in the room, but lately, Lucas had surpassed him by leaps and bounds. Maddie had elevated his brother's spirit from happy to elated.

Asher wasn't jealous. He didn't want exactly what his brother had, but he couldn't deny that the new couple made pairing up seem enticing. A few women had crossed his path over the years, but no one stuck around when they found out that the ranch was important to him and it required long work hours.

Few women wanted to play second fiddle to a field of livestock.

"I'll catch up with y'all later." Asher grabbed his hat from the rack on the way out the door. He needed some space from the happy couple, and fresh air would do him good.

Whistling an upbeat tune, he settled his hat on his head and stepped out into the cold morning. A dark-purple car was parking in front of the main house, and he waited on the porch to greet the visitor. Not many people visited the ranch besides the family and workers.

A young woman stepped out of the car, and Asher froze. Her auburn hair caught his attention first, but her uninhibited smile had his own lips turning up at the edges. She was dressed casually in jeans and a thick sweater, and he hoped she was wearing layers for this weather.

"There you are!" She closed the car door and sprinted to him, arms wide and welcoming.

Stunned, Asher opened his own arms as she bounded into him, hitting his chest and wrapping her arms around his neck.

As shocked as he was, he wrapped her in his embrace on instinct just as the stranger's lips crashed into his.

OTHER BOOKS BY MANDI BLAKE

Blackwater Ranch Series

Complete Contemporary Western Romance Series

Remembering the Cowboy

Charmed by the Cowboy

Mistaking the Cowboy

Protected by the Cowboy

Keeping the Cowboy

Redeeming the Cowboy

Blackwater Ranch Series Box Set 1-3

Blackwater Ranch Series Box Set 4-6

Blackwater Ranch Complete Series Box Set

Wolf Creek Ranch Series

Complete Contemporary Western Romance Series

Truth is a Whisper

Almost Everything

The Only Exception

Better Together

The Other Side

Forever After All

Love in Blackwater Series

Small Town Series

Love in the Storm

Love for a Lifetime

Unfailing Love Series

Complete Small-Town Christian Romance Series

A Thousand Words

Just as I Am

Never Say Goodbye

Living Hope

Beautiful Storm

All the Stars

What if I Loved You

Unfailing Love Series Box Set 1-3

Unfailing Love Series Box Set 4-6

Unfailing Love Complete Series Box Set

Heroes of Freedom Ridge Series

Multi-Author Christmas Series

Rescued by the Hero

Guarded by the Hero

Hope for the Hero

Christmas in Redemption Ridge Series

Multi-Author Christmas Series

Dreaming About Forever

Blushing Brides Series

Multi-Author Series

The Billionaire's Destined Bride

ABOUT THE AUTHOR

Mandi Blake was born and raised in Alabama where she lives with her husband and daughter, but her southern heart loves to travel. Reading has been her favorite hobby for as long as she can remember, but writing is her passion. She loves a good happily ever after in her sweet Christian romance books and loves to see her characters' relationships grow closer to God and each other.

ACKNOWLEDGMENTS

Each book I write seems like the biggest undertaking. I'm blessed to have so many friends and business partners who support me and make every book shine.

A huge thanks goes to my sister, Kenda Goforth, for being my cheerleader. Pam Humphrey, Kendra Haneline, Jenna Kelley, and Tanya Smith are the best friends and beta readers I could ask for. My editor, Brandi Aquino, pays attention to every detail when I can only see the big picture. My cover designer, Amanda Walker, always knows best, and I should just let her make all graphic design decisions.

Writing requires a lot of research, and Joleen Lawson and Melissa Taylor were kind enough to answer my unending questions about horses. My dad put up with my obscure questions about cattle because growing up on a farm didn't prepare me for the extensive knowledge needed to write this series.

I'm also blessed to be surrounded by wonderful Christian authors who encourage me every day. I never imagined that starting this writing journey would create amazing friendships at every turn.

Then there is you, the sweet reader who took a chance on this book. I pray you found an encouraging message within these pages and will stick around for more. I hope I'm able to keep on writing what I love, and you continue to enjoy the ride.

Mistaking the Cowboy

BLACKWATER RANCH BOOK 3

She kissed the wrong cowboy, but what if he was the right one?

Haley Meadows was so excited to meet the man she'd been chatting with online that she greeted him with a kiss only to find out she'd planted a big, messy, passionate wet one on his brother instead! She has to spend the rest of her vacation at Blackwater Ranch pretending like she didn't kiss the wrong cowboy and like it.

Asher Harding is knocked off his feet by an auburn haired beauty, but his infatuation is quickly squashed when he finds out she mistook him for his brother. She becomes a staple at the ranch during her visit, and getting to know her only deepens his desire for the one woman he can't have.

As Haley gets to know the Harding brothers, she finds herself torn between the one she came to meet and the one she's falling for. In the moment of truth, she'll run for the one who stole her heart.

Mistaking the Cowboy is the third book in the Christian Blackwater Ranch series, but the books can be read in any order.

Made in the USA
Coppell, TX
13 July 2024

34574853R00150